FBI
KILLER
ESCAPES

- EAST COAST IRISH TWINS
WORKED FOR J.EDGAR -

TOMMY TIERNAN

The day on the **ROCK** was icy cold, just before Christmas
when **Tommy Tiernan**,
the hardbitten **US MARINE** came face to face with
"BLACKIE BUTLER—KILLER"!

Inspired by a true story

REALITY BASED FICTION

STREAM OF CONSCIOUSNESS—COUNTY CAVAN

LIBRARY OF CONGRESS CONTROL NUMBER:		2012923625
ISBN:	HARDCOVER	978-1-4797-6766-3
	SOFTCOVER	978-1-4797-6765-6
	EBOOK	978-1-4797-6767-O

This book was printed in the United States of America.

Rev. date: 10/31/2013

To order additional copies of this book, contact:
Xlibris LLC
1-888-795-4274
www.Xlibris.com
Orders@Xlibris.com
119856

CONTENTS

PROLOGUE

CAUTION—JAMES "BLACKIE" BUTLER, the protagonist in this story, is a BOSTON $50 M DRUG KINGPIN, KILLER and TEI.

Please note, this book is "reality based fiction" and "inspired by a true story". Tommy's relatives are from County Cavan. Yes, William James, stream of consciousness writing was applied. As for any errors in spelling, grammar, and syntax, the Nun's at St. Ann's will be EXCOMMUNICATED!

The story was reduced to accommodate the readership. Original draft was 269 pages, but Playboy reviewers said too long. Why? Busy housewives, watching Dr. Phil and numerous cooking shows—FOX—news. Husbands who continue doing cow pasture pool until dark, trying to best the great one, not in his other stuff! The Shark says his sport's anti-doping procedures are "disgracefull" and blood testing needs to be instituted as soon as possible. In January, Victor used deer antler spray which is a muscle building hormone banned by the PGA Tour, detectable only by blood tests. Last, this is the first of a trilogy, need to save the hot stuff for the future installments.

CAUTION—Tommy spent entire career in Law Enforcement related professions for which he is extremely proud. Was not drafted into the military, but "dodged" the draft by becoming a United Stated Marine Corps Infantry Officer! Three years active, 20 years over all, retired as a Major. Most of his time in the Corps was in the Far East, during the Vietnam era, 58,193 American KIA's (16 in Tommy's Class) Some of Tommy's reflections since his Marine Corps service include—all Americans who are able, should make a contribution of service to the country, of at least two years. This includes the Congress, Executive Branch, State and Local pols, pro athletes, etc. The U.S. Conscription Program that was whacked in 1973, is the major contributor to our present state of affairs.

If you are a lib pol, lib professor, lib reporter, etc.—set up your book burning now! Most of you people who eschewed service for personal preferences, Tommy is greeted by their big confession—"THANKS FOR YOUR SERVICE", which wipes clean their guilt. In the `60's,—Vietnam Era—as an FBI Agent working Bank Robbers, Fugitives and 42's, he welcomed the draft dodger work for a break, from the "shooter types". You would find them, listen to the great work they hoped to do for the other Corps (Peace Corps), then print, photo and jail them. This included Dr. Benjamin, and three Boston ministers who brought 375 draft cards collected from their students for the AG! Next, the March on the Pentagon—more later.

As an FBI Agent, sworn in by J. Edgar in the DOJ room where the eight Nazi saboteur's were tried. In the Bureau, Tommy served with many other Marine Officers, who became lifetime friends. Yes, it was like moving on to the fraternities that millions of kids do every year, Tommy never had the time to play that game, but no doubt his was a bit more dangerous. Check the images of 3 of 55 Agents killed in line of duty, that were his associates. Many retired, did P.I. work, or appeared on talkies!

In the bureau, Tommy recalls the attitude was: bust them; Mirandize them; then hope the justice system, adjudicates them, especially the drug dealers, pedophiles, armed robbers, etc. Today—Investigations hindered by "POLITICAL CORRECTNESS" and more to come unless "LEADERS"—"CONGRESS AND THE EXECUTIVE BRANCH" wake up to "TERROR!"—Ft Hood, Benghazi, shoe bomber, Little Rock recruit shooting, Times Square, NY 911, and Boston Marathon 911—watch how the PC libs bounce around this one! Now the US wants to hollow out the military, why?, no real cohonez, in the Congress! WONDER WHO THE HELL IS RUNNING THE SHOW?

Well if you are across the pond and see what the non-caring US enemy is doing, what do you do? Maybe attack before all the lib professors and reporters retire. Then four American State Department employees are murdered, at Benghazi, Sept. 2012. One Secretary tells Oversight Committee, and the new one tells Congress, all is OK. We are still in the dark re last September 2012, whack job of FOUR in Benghazi, no one is above the law, as the 22 WITNESS FLAP IN WIND? Are they hoping they do a BLACKIE 16 year fade—in Mexico, Santa Monica, CA, with a visit to his old digs on the ROCK, December 21, 2007, for a Tour!

Last thought. For those that are time pressed, consider leafing through the images to get the flavor of this sordid story. Also, as the story unfolds, the Boston protagonist, JAMES "BLACKIE" BUTLER, will prove, that even though he has a serious heart condition, one really has to question if he has one—a "heart" that is! Likewise, his JERSEY SHORE nemesis, from Newark, TOMMY TIERNAN, relates some of his experiences from a career of 45 years in Public Service. The ones he does not report are either classified, or you will see them in a future novel of his trilogy. They are EAST COAST IRISH TWINS WHO WORKED FOR J. EDGAR HOOVER! SEMPER FI!—until they COLLIDED on the ROCK!

PAY ATTENTION—

WHO ALMOST GETS WHACKED ON THE ROCK?

WHAT IS THE SECRET TO 15 YEAR VACATION?

WAS SANTA MONICA, REALLY AN FBI BUST?

SAVE FRIDAY AFTERNOONS FOR—91'S—?

THANKS

Special thanks from the author to the many relatives near and far for their support and inspiration. There was an extensive and intensive security review, including political correctness, which resulted in the deletion of numerous items. Also, a number were top secret classified. The "thank you" includes—ALL MARINES, FBI AGENTS, PUBLIC SAFETY OFFICERS, TEACHERS AND COACHES AT ST. ANN'S, EAST SIDE, AND THE "HALL", MALIBU, SEAN, BILL, RUSH and MARK! Also, thanks to Connie, Randy, Bob, Malibu, Pete, Brooke, David, Shep, White, Mom and Dad, The CLARK GANG, the Brooklyn Dodgers, Vince and all the Nuns.

Finally, thanks for the inspiration for this story goes to the IRA—IRISH RAT ASSHOLE, BLACKIE, the East Coast Twin who worked for J. Edgar? Along with the alleged nineteen plus whack jobs, the BOSTON DRUG KINGPIN, obliterated the lives of thousands of Boston citizens and youth, as he became a millionaire, many times over! Thank God, the FBI and locals, more than rose to the occasion for the events of Patriots Day—2013. Question is—HOW MANY MORE ARE OUT THERE?

FOREWORD

Just a little background on the principals in this reality based fiction, which is inspired by true events! The County Cavan application is in recognition of William James from County Cavan, and his contribution to literature—'stream of consciousness'! You will see, as the story unfolds, Tommy Tiernan, the nemesis, and Blackie Butler, the protagonist, play out the stream, in their own unique fashion, as applied by their Cavan cousin.

Before we launch, a moment of reflection for the Elite Team of 19 Firefighters that perished in the AZ "Wildfire", that took them just before Independence Day—2013. To keep in perspective the 19 deaths, which equals the number of whack jobs that our protagonist, **BLACKIE**—has been charged with as the Boston DRUG Kingpin and Winter Hill Gang Boss. BUT, for BLACKIE, his real money—$50 M plus was from DRUGS. Check the most recent **Health of Boston Report, Substance Abuse—for Boston Residents,** the numbers are absolutely staggering! BUT, why do not the City Fathers—Mothers, get upset and push the city. Are they stupid—complicit—corrupt? The problem is out there, the kids continue to hit the dirt—buried—but no one really gives a DAMN! The Winter Hill BLACKIE—DRUG deals went on for a couple decades, and were ignored by the Feds, States and locals, all who were hunting down those bad MAFIA guys! While BLACKIE was on his government aided 16 year vacation, the business flourished with his replacements, and more DEAD Boston young!

This same deal continues all over the country! The DRUG guy sets up in a locale, the druggies then gravitate to the source, just like BLACKIE did in BOSTON—SOUTHIE, and become millionaires. Next, is the local payoffs. Look at the BLACKIE process, it shows how it works. NOW, look at any DRUG PROGRAMS in the US, they are all exactly the same. The solution—legalize drugs? Although with the direction of pro sports, maybe we missed the boat!

OK—With this intro, pay attention as this story unfolds and addresses serious payoffs at all levels, in local and Fed programs. By now we all have heard in the press about the local corruption in Boston, please keep in mind the Fed chain of command wends its way to HQ—WDC. Promise you will not be surprised to learn that the BN OC guy took orders from HQ, possibly a Nam draft dodger! Note—the 19 whack jobs will not get attention in this story, which are available in local reports and books. The focus is all the young DRUG deaths, that the RAT caused, a number who were his relatives!

As the first chapter launches, you will become acquainted with Tommy Tiernan. He hails from Irish—German stock. His journey starts in Newark, N.J., and moves to various international locations in Europe and the Far East. He is the oldest of five boys. Dad and Mom provided the inspiration for all to excel, no matter what the obstacles and challenges! All family members made contributions as expected. These were made with a high level of sacrifice. While Dad and Mom, never had the chance to graduate from college, all five of Tommy's Fire Team are college graduates, and beyond—lawyer, couple Masters, etc.

Tommy's Fire Team, lived in the Ironbound section—Down-neck—, on the other side of the tracks! For those who know the area, it was in the shadow of Ruppert Stadium and the Ballentine Brewery. Time frame—Tommy arrived just prior to the "big war"! The number was increased by a WWII uncle, who lived with him, went to Seton Hall on GI Bill, and Grandma till she passed, with countless beagles!

Career started as a paper boy. Carried the Star Ledger and the Evening News! After first year saved enough for a newer bike. The guy down the street with mob connections, truck driver, next to the corner tavern, seemed like every corner had them for the thirsty populace! Said the brand new Schwinn—knee action fell off a truck! Had the coolest bike in the hood. Younger Fire Team was envious, "hard work".

Did the altar boy tour at local St. Ann's Church. Same as Machine Gun Kelly did on the ROCK, being Irish he knew where the wine was kept. As oldest in the gang, urged Mom and Dad to be romantic so we could get more batting practice fielders. Results—Tommy makes All-City and County Baseball Teams, and Seton Hall offers him a D-1 student-athlete scholarship. He and the Fire Team celebrated at the iconic Tom Farley's bar, next to the Ballantine Brewery!

The Brooklyn Dodgers, Tommy's team forever, in a letter from Al Campanis invited him to Ebbets Field for a tryout with the Brooklyn Dodger Rookies. He was on the bench with the World Champions—1955—Preacher, Campy, Hodges (WW II—Okinawa—Marine), Robinson, PeeWee, Cox, Furillo, Snider, and Cimoli. Yes, Dad the Fire Captain by now, said good example for your Fire Team. Well, there is no doubt in Tommy's mind, the long BP made a difference. And, one of the team said, had he batted Lefty, he could make the show!

One day batting Lefty, he hit the ball on the Ruppert roof—about 450 plus! Tommy regrets that none of his coaches urged him to switch hit. Maybe his favorite nun, Miriam, got to them—no lefty! Back story—Tommy's favorite nun insisted, no writing Lefty, so when you did you got the three sided ruler treatment! What did it do to Tommy's motor centers, a plus for the upcoming tests at Marine Corps and FBI? The hike from the house to the ball yard took about 40 minutes. It was around some unusual shaped blocks, under Rt 1 near the Pulaski Skyway, the rest of the route was Wilson Ave, around the Stadium to Ironbound Field. As we rounded the corner, we could hear the old stadium bricks groan, "here they come again"! The ball field, loaded with rocks and broken glass was a sight, but no one else there, so free for the Fire Team plus one.

Just beyond the right field area was a local dump. They did not know it at the time, but in future years all these areas were declared Super Toxic Dumps! Guess Tommy will make it, he later survived the polluted SF Bay, Alcatraz and Gate swims, with WW II munitions sunk all around the ROCK. Incentive for Fire Team, after BP was rat hunting. The dump was a great spot for hunting rats with the Red Ryder bb guns,after batting practice, five shots with the youngest first!

A special event would occur on Friday night. Tommy would finish his papers, go by Vince's pizza place, get the biggest pizza, loaded with cheese, and pedal home, no delivery trucks, plus $. Down to the basement, with the Gillette fights on a 13-inch B/W TV.—No colored TV invented yet. One of the team, in fact it may have been the one who later became a lawyer, was seen skipping his crust so he could get more pizza. HALT—Violation of fair pizza eating! For remainder of month he got the clean up duty.

As a Seton Hall Alum, with 45 years in law enforcement, Tommy wants to put in a plug for another Hall guy with the NY State Prison Board. Denis Kozlowski, never did harm to anyone, with his recent work with Veterans, time to release him! Send him to NJ Corrections Dept., to consult/manage, per NY Times Dec-2012.

Probably fortified with the pizza, two months before Ebbets and the Hall, Tommy shattered two long standing Newark City swimming records, in the Fly and the Medley. At the Hall, Tommy was the Captain and MVP on the swim team, doing Fly and Free! Hall of Fame at Hall?—applied— Frosh, b4th-.405,-18rbi, Then bullpen, Swim Team Capt/ MVP, "Silence"! Down the road, when assigned to the left coast, he took on the Gate and Alcatraz. Tommy is the **"ONLY FBI AGENT EVER"** to swim Alcatraz to SF—and Golden Gate North & South (passing kidney stones)—all swims, no wet suit (did not own one), water temp and age 55, swirling currents, SHARKS?—South End Rowing Club!

Yes, FOUR of the Team of Brothers, were Marine Corps Officers during the Vietnam era, serving in the Far East. Two were 0302, Infantry and Recon, one Amtraks, and one Artillery. All FOUR passed the rugged Marine Officer boot camps and graduated from The Basic School, Quantico, Va. Later, TWO of the four graduated as FBI Special Agents, Basic

Training, from, you guessed it, the FBI Academy, Quantico, Va. The team often thanks Tommy for recruiting them into the Marine Corps!

Special thanks to Brooke, for her encouragement and support, who's Mom was a resident of the Ironbound section of Newark, N.J. Her dad was a VP at the Ballantine Brewery. At the Inaugural for President George Herbert Walker Bush, Brooke and her Mom had their personal security provided by Tommy! After all, she was a recent grad of Princeton, Tommy a Marine, FBI guy from the Seton "Hall". She said she loved Marines from the Ironbound! Somehow a tennis player aced Tommy out?

DEDICATED TO ALL WHO SERVED

AND DID NOT "DODGE" !

IN REMEMBRANCE TO BOSTON'S DEAD

For those Boston residents, and their relatives, that Blackie is alleged to have whacked AND the Southie youngsters that got hooked on drugs, as he became a millionaire, they became vegetables !—Michael Milarno 1973, Al Plummer 1973, William O'Brien 1973, James O'Toole 1973, Al Notorangeli 1974, James Sousa 1974, Paul McGonagl 1974, Edward Connors 1975, Thomas King 1975, Francis Leonard 1975, Richard Castucci 1976, Roger Wheeler 1981, Debra Davis 1981, Brian Holloran 1982, Michael Donohue 1982, John Calahan 1982, Arthur Barret 1983, John McIntyre 1984, Deborah Hussey 1985, James William Lawlor 2007, LA,—that we know of—.

PRESENTATION & DISCUSSION

BY TOMMY TIERNAN

— ONE HOUR, PER SUBJECT, Q & A

— MARINE CORPS

— FBI

— ALCATRAZ—MYSTERIES

— FBI KILLER ESCAPES, ETC.

— CONTACT PUBLICIST
shu25@sbcglobal.net

CHAPTER I

THE MARINES
LAW ENFORCEMENT

It was that time of year for the FOURTH of JULY—INDEPENDENCE DAY PARADE and CELEBRATION! Tommy Tiernan was a member of the First Marine Division unit. VINCE RIOS—THE VIETNAM MARINE CORPS WAR HERO was a participant. He was a regular ever since losing both legs and his lower right arm to an IED! Yes, he was in a wheel chair that was powered by what remained of his left hand! Tommy Tiernan met Vince and Steve to brief them on the parade at the iconic "HARPOON LOUIES", in San Francisco the week before the parade. They were serviced by some fine looking MARINE CORPS-E-4'S-Ladies of course. The Marine Corps Drum and Bugle Corps, Camp Pendleton, CA., played as their prep for the Rose Bowl Parade. At the end of the parade, all celebrated at McGOVERN'S, and the BROADWAY in appropriate MARINE CORPS fashion! "THE

MARINE CORPS HYMN", "SEMPER FI" and "Ooh-rah" all night!

Yes, on this day the parades and fireworks draw numerous Americans to the City Square to celebrate Freedom and Independence—NEWS ALERT—Six more Americans wounded in Afghanistan by IED! Pols—Federal, State and local tell us how great they are, and express their thanks for all who "served"! This despite the fact that almost NONE of them know from experience what "served" means. For them you may notice their lapel American flags have been replaced by House and Senate buttons, probably provided by the "K" St. lobby crowd. When asked, the Pols say no "service" yet, BUT they are members of the Congressional—Executive Branch "Thanks for your Service" Carcass!

This is the same Fed group that commits the "voluntary" military to war. When the limbless, etc return they oversee the VA for their care. Most VA offices are at least six months behind. The Secretary and Undersecretary of VA should be **FIRED NOW!** Why—how can you not act if the Titanic is sinking! So hire one of your DOD contractors to run it—not obamacare. Mean time, put the VA IG in charge. Take time from your golf dates to check the stats—suicides skyrocketing, etc. The families that are left home, fall apart, especially with 3 and 4 rotations. Yes, you Feds have looked the other way, since 1973, it is time to show some guts and **WAKE UP!** Politicians—Federal, State and local, show up to express their thanks, even though most "never served". They will be front and center, American Flags in their lapel, thanking all for their "service". In 1973, they buried the draft, which now has rotations going to the war zone constantly. Result—suicides have skyrocketed! The families that are left home, fall apart.

Yes, you Feds have looked the other way, since 1973, it is time to **WAKE UP!**

Another issue you must address, IED's. Both the wars produced numerous lost limbs, as the Congress and DOD tried to decide what to do! The limbs from the troops should be mounted around the Washington Monument, as a constant reminder to the Congress and the Administration, what you did to them. Not unlike what you did during Vietnam, 58,193 KIA's. Yes, we have bombers that could have whacked the enemy IED issue. Visit VA hospitals, as Tommy has done at Palo Alto Vets, if you need a dose of reality. When are you going to rip away from the Feds, some of the green money, and redirect it to the VA or the Wounded Warrior Project. With the drop off in enlistments, you better re-think your 1973 vote. Unless you plan to let the Peace Corps get back in to the picture. In the past we had pro-athletes, who served, like Warren Spahn, winningest lefty ever, Bronze Star—Purple Heart, Battle of Bulge, and two Marines. Ted Williams and Jerry Coleman, both, two wars. More on this later. As the American ballplayers are drafted in the military, the teams would continue to play with the numerous foreign players now on the roster and in the minors.

BACKGROUND OF EAST COAST IRISH TWINS WHO WORKED FOR J.EDGAR BLACKIE BUTLER—TOMMY TIERNAN

Records indicate that BLACKIE, protagonist, served in the Air Force, during the '50's. While his nemesis, Tommy, was a Vietnam era, Marine Corps, Infantry Platoon Officer, in the Far East; while BLACKIE did 3 years on the ROCK for a series of Bank jobs. Point is, we are all free to choose our own paths. Maybe BLACKIE'S youth was marked by abuse, addiction, personality, or bi-polar disorders. Some say he had a brother who was powerful in the Boston and Massachusetts. Go figure, why one had good seeds and the other was a RAT! The ROCK was closed soon after he left, not because of him, probably the Morris-Anglin escape. Maybe Blackie helped in the escape, Blackie may know where they are in South America, probably in Cuzo, Peru as Tour Directors of Amazon rain forest of Peru. Check Alcatraz display at FBI office in San Francisco for postcard to Warden from escapees, thanking HIM!

Around 1965, with the help of a Southie school buddy Blackie was recruited to help the Bureau break up the LCN Boston mob! At that time, Tommy was on the BR and Fugitive Squad in NYO, having first been assigned to train bombings, fugitives, Klan bank robbery in Jacksonville. So we now have these two East Coast Irishmen, pursuing different paths, not knowing that they would **"COLLIDE"** on the ROCK, before the Boston Red Sox would beat the Brooklyn Dodgers!

Tommy Tiernan's last tour of duty was as the Regional Inspector General, for the U. S. Department of Justice based in San Francisco, CA. The office he directed covered the Western U S for all Department of Justice Offices. They investigated the: INS,FBI, DEA, BOP, USMS, OJP, USA, and BP. Just before 9/11, Tommy was directed to do a major investigation of the INS. For this effort he was provided his pick of staff from all offices. He was required to fly into WDC on New Year's Day. He got to his favorite Virginia watering hole, just in time to see the Rose Bowl at Theisman's!

Next day, over to the Main Justice with his boss to get the review under way. Advised AG wanted a thorough multi-level and multi-office review of INS, and whether they met there goals and objectives. Completed report to be on the AG's desk by Valentine's Day. You guessed it, from that day on, we referred to the report as the Valentine's Day Massacre! Never learned the truth, but the AG and the INS Director had issues. May have been the behavior of the INS Western Regional Director, who secretly had made a major film about his Region, without AG approval. Word was he worked it out with his old Hollywood buddies. The INS Director resigned by Memorial Day!

While at HQ, one of Tommy's contacts asked for his security assistance at the Inaugural Ball for President Bush. The President arrived just after attending the Medal of Honor Ball, at the Hilton! His mandatory attendance was for ALL Presidents similar to George Washington. The INS job was going well, with staff reporting in daily. The Ball was at Washington Convention Center. Thousands of people, four bands, 15 bars! Given his Marine Officer background, Athletic prowess, sworn in by J.Edgar—he was security for the Oak Ridge Boys and a fellow Newark resident—not Whitney, but Brooke and her

Mom! In her mid twenties, just graduated, Princeton U and looked fantastic! She said she loved Newark Marines! It seemed like everyone there asked for her autograph, she turned down no one. She would ask for their program, then name, and wrote a note, and then signed it! We got her back to Georgetown by curfew! Also at the Ball, Izzy Goldfine, Newark—S. F. bookie, who worked with Hugh Addonizio, at Yardville. Joe Horne, French Foreign Legion attended with Brooklyn Louie, Kevin, Chuck and Whelan.

BLACKIE FLASHBACK

BLACKIE screamed! "Instead of killing you, we will buy the store." Blackie said in the paper bag, was $67,000 in cash. The Jakes had put out about $100,000 for the South Boston Liquor Mart, but instead of killing you, we will buy the store! He was the mob boss of the Winter Hill Gang, and heavily connected with the Bureau. The role, would run for many years, and would allow for numerous drug crimes/homicides. When he left Boston, it was no surprise, for he left behind a mess that dwarfed the Brinks Robbery. All covered up by his Top Informant role with the Bureau.

Best we know, 19 homicides, including two females he knew and sort of dated, that he strangled to death. Countless humans who were hooked on drugs, never to have a life, and condemned to death, because this RAT made millions from the drugs he sold. Dealers had to pay rent on every gram of Santa Claus, code name for coke. Young men, even some mothers, were selling drugs out of their homes—angel dust, mescaline, valium, speed, coke and heroin. Did the press ever dig into this story, no they wanted to do the homicides and the corruption. BUT, the people that were dead, they can't talk, the media comments from a couple druggies and that is it! Where were the investigative journalists? Maybe they were out to lunch, like the Red Sox!

A little background on Tommy Tiernan, that you may not know. Tommy's home town was Newark, NJ. He was the oldest of family of five boys. Dad a fireman, Mom was a teacher at the local Catholic School. Tommy had a dream, to excel in sports, especially in baseball and swimming! Goal—the Brooklyn Bums, swim in Olympics! Inspired by his parents, and two uncles who served their country in WW II. One on the Third Wave at Normandy, the other a Navy CPO, in the Pacific, etc.

Next stop was the local American Legion Club, where membership continues to decline. Reason, attitude of the younger generation and the Congressional "spineless" whack job in 1973, when they killed the Draft. Yes, Vietnam was mismanaged, and was the beginning of US downfall! It gave a boost to the Peace Corps, and the rest ran off to Canada!

The effect was to "disenfranchise" millions of Americans from the opportunity to serve their country, in the spirit of George Washington, for the rest of their lives! Their main participation in the country, is what they send to the IRS! The concept of participation in the program of "conscription" is not part of their vocabulary, but they all know they should pay their dues. Conscription is one piece of a multifaceted approach to pulling us together for the long haul. The Fed government gave them a pass. Today, about two percent of the citizens serve, while the other 98 per cent watch the TV news reports on the limbless hero's who return. Military enlistments are in the tank! We need more than Liberty and Tyranny, for our younger generation to embrace USA.

No, I am not advocating wars, but if we commit to a National Service of two years, Public Service or Military Service, we will know and care more about the US. We will have a strong commitment to the country, and we can take a knowledgeable shot at the Congress that commits us to winless wars, with multiple rotations. Why, having been even a small part of the military and/or service to the US, it will give all an entitlement to leverage the Congress and Administration to a reasonable direction, on military and other issues.

We then do not leave it exclusively to the non-serving talking heads, who have never walked the walk! Watch them on the Sunday talk shows, not one of them has military background, BUT they have all the answers, notably the great generation rep! The military, amounts to about 2 percent of the US population, while the 98 per cent watch it on TV, or from the ninth hole! Yes, there are very dark clouds ahead! BENGHAZI—FOUR DEAD AMERICANS, ISRAEL, GAZA, MIDDLE-EAST, CHINA on the rise! NOW—Rules of Engagement!

Since the Congressional whack job, two winless wars by the Administration. If we stacked up the loss of limbs, it would far exceed the Washington Monument! The Congress appears to care less. Why? In Tommy's opinion, maybe 5 per cent of the Congress and Hill staffers have participated in Public or Military Service, so most are "dodgers", but if we all served, two years, we all would really care! TRY IT!

Tommy goes to Palo Alto VA and hears the stories! Tommy has a Marine buddy, Vince lost two legs and a right arm to a

IED in Vietnam! Has wheel chair behind his pickup truck seat, never complains. After Nam, he got his AA, BA, and MA, pretty much on his own. Why is it that the Sunday talking heads show never includes a military rep, with ten years of war, military cuts coming, and Iran developing nuclear weapons. Israel, now defending itself, after asking for US assistance—refused. The China military build up may soon position them much closer to our Left Coast shores, and the welcoming to Half Moon Bay landing beaches! First, cancel Mavericks "Nobody likes to fight. But somebody has to know how. We're looking for a few good men/women", is the recruiting theme for the **United States Marine Corps**!

Last year, at the Marines Memorial Club, SF, Sec Def said, we do not need two armies, no more Marine Corps landings, so we plan to cut the Corps numbers in half, on the way to complete disestablishment! Then SecDef said he plans to retire and "thanks for your service"! He did not even flinch when he made the comments! But, that attitude speaks volumes for the Administration and the Congress!

The first MARINE recruiter was Captain Samuel Nicholas. In 1775, on the eve of the Revolution, he signed up volunteers to serve as sharpshooters on the Navy ship, Black Prince. His recruiting office was Tun Tavern in Philadelphia, the cradle of Liberty!

Fifty years ago, on November 10, Tommy Tiernan was sworn in to the **MARINE** Officer Candidate Program (PLC). This was done at the Recruiting Station on lower Broadway, NYC, a few blocks from "Ground Zero"! **SEMPER FI!**

TOMMY FIRETEAM FLASHBACK

As a Lt in the USMC, Tommy was approached by his brothers about volunteering. His response, don't take the "sissy" Peace Corps route, like so many have done, but he asked, **"Want to serve with the best". DONE!** And the rest is history! They grew up in the Ironbound, around the corner from the Ballentine Brewery and Bears Ruppert Stadium (1926-1967), Newark Bears and Newark Eagles (Negro League) both associated with the New York Yankees. The Stadium saw Zale level Graziano, in the 3rd of their final fight.

A Marine platoon has 3 squads of 13, and each squad has 3 fire teams, Tommy's **FIRE TEAM** (4 man Marine fighting unit), rooted for Mantle, Ford, Yogi etc, the others hung with Hodges, Robinson, Snider, Cimoli, Ebbets Field, and the Bums!

The four were the **USMC** Vietnam era, Feb 1961 to May 1975, **TOMMY FIRE TEAM—**

TOMMY—1960-1963, Infantry Platoon Commander, 3rdMarDiv, Gd Officer, NAD, OK;

PADRIG—1963-1966, Infantry Platoon Commander, Force Recon, 3rd/2nd MarDiv;

BERNIE—1966-1969 Commander Motor T, Artillery, RVN, Gd Officer, NAD, NJ;

CAVAN—1970-1973 Commander AM Tracks, RVN, Camp Pendleton, CA;

Yes, they are "**THE ONLY FOUR BROTHERS**" to serve as **MARINE OFFICERS**, during the Vietnam era! And, all four brothers graduated from **THE BASIC SCHOOL,** "making Marine Corps History for one family"!

QUANTICO, VA SEMPER FI!

Tommy was commissioned in June and had orders for Marine Corps Basic School, at Quantico, VA., in September. That meant he would have to spend the entire summer on the "Jersey Shore" as an Atlantic Ocean Lifeguard. One of his swim buddies suggested Seaside Heights, NJ had open slots. This is the place "Snookie" made her Olympic debut! At that time Tommy guarded her Mom and Snok was a youngin!

Guards work hours—0900 to 1800. Daily workouts, first a mile swim in ocean, then partner with Guido for a 2 mile row in the Guard boat, followed by pushups, sit ups. Guido was a weight lifter and when we hit the bench the young honey's were hanging close and asking if they could put their blankets near his chair. Yeah, Guido could not handle all of them so he and Tommy got to flip coins, for the night time hooters! Not the real "hooters".—Had not been invented yet!

Given Tommy's likeness to Tab, the sweetie's called him Tab! Often at night, he would put moves on them at the "Chatter Box", Bar/Dance Club, on the boards. With these ladies, Tommy never had to pay for anything! Suzy had approached Tommy during one of his beach guard walks. Said she had been checking him out, she came to the Heights from Quogue, and had her new pink blanket that she wanted to christian with Tommy, "guard work" is **HELL**!

Nancy was very attractive, and great smile/body to match! She was from Short Hills, just graduated from Princeton, Philosophy major. She remembered the Basketball scandal at Tommy's Big East school, where he was a D-1, student-athlete. Two players were busted for shaving points, Tommy was pre-law, they were PE, he knew them, the one from LA had a problem, had trouble reading! Terri had a problem, **p**assing epistemology, until she agreed to sleep with her professor, Lilly! Another blanket christened?

Second day on the bench, got some good advice from Guido. He said make sure you let them swallow! At first I thought he was talking about the hooters! No, it is the swimmers, they have not been in water all winter, now at the beach, ocean drop off is very steep, so . . . .! Let them swallow first or they will go right back in ocean. Guido had it right! It cut the saves in half, more time to watch for sharks!, and our night time entertainment. Guido was from Down Neck, Hawkins St School, near Ballantine Brewery. Also, Tom Farley's bar was near Ballantine's brewery. His requirement was if you could see over the bar he would serve you. Back in the dark corner, there were some uniform cops, from 3rd Precinct, dealing with their thirst!

After an exemplary career in the Marine Corps, and the FBI, he had a chance to escape the WDC heat and humidity. Tommy accepted a position on the West Coast as the SF Inspector General for the Department of Justice. He often tells colleagues, his best job ever, was as an Agent-Lifeguard. But, location, left coast, and better pay, won out! Remember, that was soon after a commendation from the Big Boss!

Tommy said it was now time to head to the coast and crash at the Ritz, over looking the Pacific Ocean. One of Tommy's lady friends had a special room at the hotel, where she was a bartender at the Waves Bar! Tommy had checked with Terri from the American Legion, she said you all come! He had been helping Terri, from Philly, prepare for her upcoming Golden Gate swim. She was planning to be the first to swim it in a bikini! It is the same suit she wears in her room when they are together talking about proper stroking techniques! Also, in college she was a philosophy major so we often discussed logic and epistemology, as she flings off her pink thing! Then, nude with a golden tan, big green eyes, she unfolded a new green blanket! Question, Tommy do you want to, "Make My Day ", here—or down at the beach! How about a double header, here first, then down to the beach with a few Margarita's. Terri had started at DOJ, after Penn State, as the Main Justice photographer!

Next morning, we headed up the freeway early to get the special parking. As we left the South End Rowing Club for our swim workout at Aquatic Park in the SF Bay, the sun was splashing on the Golden Gate Bridge, to the West. The day had broken very cold and gray. By the time we finished, in two hours, the sun was glistening off Alcatraz, the ROCK, to the east, the first Super-Max Fed Lockup, 1934.

We went by the Senior's facility and said hello to Gunner. He was a retired Pilot Boat Captain from Norway, and had served with the Navy in the Bay in WW II. He was setting up tables for seniors, in the North Beach area of SF, did this on a daily basis. It overlooked the Aquatic Park area, with the ROCK, the Golden Gate Bridge, and the San Francisco Skyline as background!

The Bay swim with Bob, Frank, Randy and Phil, was part of training for the Alcatraz swims! Also, swim workouts at

Elks Lodge where he was life member along with the Jewish Community Center. We had already agreed to meet at the Buena Vista or the Taddich Grill for brunch, where a staffer from a Washington, D. C., Oversight and Government Reform Committee, would join us! If reservations were tight, the backup, Lefty O'Douls!

Tommy was a long time member of the South End Rowing Club est 1873, at Aquatic Park. He swam in the Bay near the Balclutha, a turn of the century three masted Square-Rigger, that is open for tourists. His father-in-law, Jim, sailed the ship as a Sea Scout, LA to San Diego, when he was 15 years old! Tommy donated the Ship's Log that his Father-in-Law, gave him, to the San Francisco Maritime Museum curator.

The Balclutha is a steel ship built in Glasglow in 1886, seven years before SERC. She engaged in grain hauling and later in trans-Pacific lumber trade as the Star of Alaska. Through 1930 she was a cannery supply vessel for the Alaska Packer Assn. In 1934, the San Francisco Maritime Museum purchased the ship. The Hyde St Pier is the permanent location for the Balclutha, on Aquatic Park near the Dolphin & South End Rowing Club, both established in the late 1800's.

Jim worked mostly for Lockheed in southern California. His later career, was in Las Vegas, working for Howard Hughes, stories? On occasion he took Tommy by the green shed to see Howard's Spruce Goose. As a youngster, Jim lived in Compton, his Dad was a Shell oil worker from Scotland. Jim at 15, was in a Sea Scout Troop.

This being Depression time, just before WW II, no real boats to sail. So they made boats out of paper and had operations on dining room tables. One day five Scouts went to

Long Beach Harbor by bike. They were approached by Frank Kissinger, from Marin, CA and owner of the Balclutha. He said he needed a crew to sail it to San Diego for an upcoming Exibition! Not stated, he needed to get out of LA, cause he was way behind on Port fees.

The Sea Scouts all voted a big "yes", to make trip, none had a cel phone to check at home (yet to be invented). None had ever been out to sea, none were Marines but they wanted the challenge! One of them, Larry, would later become the 1st Mate for 10 years for Humphrey on his 55ft yawl named the Santana, out of Newport, CA. Larry was very sick when Tommy talked to him, because of lung cancer. He used to bum smokes from Humphrey, who died of lung cancer. But, what stories, he shared with Tommy about the Santana, and Humphrey!

BLACKIE FLASHBACK

BLACKIE was indicted around the holidays and so he decided it was a good time to think about leaving the Red Sox part of the country, and head out to Dodger territory. Not sure which "handler" gave him vacation planning help. Rumor has it he considered having the Feds get him placed in the Peace Corps. He did recruit a traveling companion, female type, Carol to help him read maps. He was too cheap to get an automatic car map, GPS, he thought it would be bugged! Had his guns and money in the trunk, with his Batman comic books, no Dick Tracy! Dropped Stan at Chili's and got Carol at Malibu, and headed south. Stan began to help the Bureau, so BLACKIE changed to Thomas F. Baxter alias, who passed in 1979.

Tommy always wondered what he was swimming over during his Gate swims! The Golden Gate Bridge today, is caressed by the same fogs that obscured the Gate for centuries. The same river of fresh water, draining the same 40 percent of the land mass of the interior, still rushes westward through the Gate, at the rate of more than half a million cubic feet per second in winter months, a greater flow than the Colorado River. The same Pacific, twice a day, pours its 2.3 million cubic feet of salt water per second through the channel for twenty minutes, twice in a twenty-four hour cycle.

Under the surface of the water, the same fish, seals, and sea lions continue to swim in and out of the Gate that nourishes them, and the same snakes crawl along the sea floor. The oyster beds, which fed generations of native americans and flourished in the early 20th century—when a young Jack London earned money as an oyster pirate!

Whenever Tommy saw the Golden Gate Bridge it reminded him of his return from the Far East as a Marine Corps Platoon Commander. Why?, he left San Diego on a troop ship, 21 days to Japan, now return to SF on a 707, first US site he saw was Golden Gate, en route to Travis AFB. His Uncle Gene saw it on his return from WW II. His last invasion was Okinawa, as a Navy Chief, and he barely survived the Jap kamikaze attacks!

On Hickam AFB stopover, got caught up with Robert Gerard and some of his knockout female security guards. We all did the Military Hale Koa dinner, then the Beach Bar with Suzie, Marine Buck Sgt from West Palm. As the music from the bar, Sweet Caroline, and a collection of Beach Boy's, under a full moon with Suzie who loved to skinny dip! She also had a red beach blanket that we eventually christened.

Her fit bronzed body glowed in the full moon light! Tommy caught up on sleep on the 707, till the glistening Golden Gate Bridge came into view!

BLACKIE FLASHBACK

Meanwhile, **BLACKIE** in Boston, at work doing his business and adding to kill #'s. Mack, was a boat driver, with the Irish Curse, busted for DUI, and talked about helping his relatives in Ireland with some guns—like **"Fast and Furious"**. Problem, BLACKIE the TE rat learned about it . . . from? Mack was on the dirt basement floor, tortured by being choked with BLACKIE pulling a rope to the right and Shotgun pulling to the left, then a bullet in his forehead, little blood because he was dead when shot. Next burial in the basement. His teeth were pulled with pliers, you could hear the teeth separating from the jawbone. BLACKIE, had an orgasm while watching Mack die, climaxed in his pants, so went upstairs to lie down and rest! Yes, Blackie was both a psychopath and sociopath and not someone you wanted your sister to date! Also, he is a serial killer, who enjoyed homosexual and pedophile conquests, with his gold chain dangling! Just ask Sal the astronaut!

When Gene returned home from the War, he lived with Tommy. Dad was a Fire Capt. at that time, Tommy had two younger brothers, on way to five boys. Quarters were tight, but somehow they managed. Gene used the GI Bill to get a college degree, then County probation officer. He was able to do some pitching at Seton Hall, but with school studies he also played in the Ironbound Twilight League. The park was next to the Newark Bears Stadium, the perennial International League Champs and part of the NY Yankees Organization.

Yes, there was another Uncle, Benny was in the Army, and landed on the Third Wave at Normandy. After the War, he became a Newark Policeman. He was an All-Star Semi-Pro first baseman and lived on the same block as Tommy. With the urging of his parents and two Uncles, Tommy set his academic and athletic goals. As a Senior at East Side High, Tommy was elected the school's Student Council President. On Sundays, Uncle Benny would round up the fire team for BP at Riverbank Park.

In recent years, Tommy won over 100 swim medals in Masters, World Police and Fire Games. Also, as a member of the SERC, he swam the Golden Gate Bridge, North and South (kidney stones) and Alcatraz to SF twice, without a wet suit (did not own one), in treacherous currents, two miles, and age and temp about 55! Swims over an hour, shark escort—Great Whites! No other Special Agent has ever done what Tommy did! None of the 36 convict escape attempts from Alcatraz were successful, 5—are still missing, Lee Morris, Anglin brothers, 1962; Roe and Cole 1937.

While Tommy never made the Olympics, he did beat an Olympic Gold Medalist, **PARRY O'BRIEN, i**n a Master's 50 Free, at Stanford University! Shot Put, GOLD—Helsinki—1952 and Melbourne—1956. He was from, BLACKIE'S hiding place (?), Santa Monica, and USC! **SEMPER FI**! This GOLD is treasured the most by Tommy, and he would like to talk to BLACKIE about his putting it in his vault for safe keeping with the his tapes and comic books.

As HS senior in swimming, Tommy shattered two long standing Newark records, **i**n Fly and Medley. Tommy did his summer swim training in the Newark Bay, and at a public pool that he got to by jumping freight trains, that ran a block behind his house. The tough part was jumping off at the end. The freight would gain speed and the jump was into corse coke! In later years, all these areas were declared by the EPA to be Toxic Waste Dumps, not to be confused with MK-ULTRA!

Three months after swims, he shattered two swim records and Tommy made the **All-City/County Baseball Team!** The Dodgers invited him to Ebbets Field for a tryout, for the Dodger Rookies! Tommy sat next to the "Boys of Summer", who beat the Yanks, in the 1955 World Series—combine of Branch Rickey and Al Campanis launched Tommy on an enviable career path.

—Roy Campanella, Gil Hodges, Jackie Robinson, PeeWee Reese, Billy Cox, Carl Furillo, Duke Snider, and Gino Cimoli! Tommy was a lifer "Brooklyn" Dodger fan! After tryout, a Big East college, Seton Hall, NJ, offered him **a D-1, student athlete ride!** Yes, for Tommy sports, hard work and goals, opened doors to a world that he did not know even existed. The rest is history! Except, younger brother, who was a great ball player once said, you big lug, had you batted Lefty, you would have made the show!!

Batted 4th, .405 as Frosh, with 18 RBI's, then he was asked to help in the pen! Finished up as the Captain and MVP on the Swim Team. Only student athlete to letter in two major sports during career, still awaiting recognition by his Big East college. Ironbound? Monsignor? Or maybe it was his wake up call, as pre-law at end of first year, GPA had him back on the docks! Unless he took two summer courses, and got B's. The athlete took the challenge and boosted his GPA!, and stayed at the Hall! Close call.

Hofstra University on LI, was the Hall opponent. Tommy was asked by his swim coach, to take team to Hofstra College for meet. It was their homecoming, and they expected a turnout. Some parts of this story are sworn to secrecy, NCAA statue of limitations! Coach gave Tommy the gas and food money. The drive to the Island was over the George Washington bridge, near the famous Yankee Stadium, Tommy's enemy. We met at the Newark Athletic Club, in the Military Park Hotel. Coach Jim took the Prep team to Philadelphia, for a big meet. They won!

Tommy knew he might come up short on swimmers, and at this location he might be able to recruit some help. At the pool were team members, also a number of High School swimmers from a local team, that won the NJ State Championship. Problem—the HS guys were Jewish with the star of David on their neck chains. Told them they needed to park their medals, as he gave them Irish names and gas and food money for the meet. As a Catholic Altar boy, this was a major success, for Judeo-Christian relations!

As the meet went on, and the score was tied, the Hofstra coach asks Tommy about the "new swimmers" from last year. Well, Tommy had to make sure his guys did not WIN, the meet, or an NCAA investigation! Yes, Tommy set up the event swimmers, including the last relay, meet tied, that Tommy anchored. OPPS, he left too soon and forfeited the last relay. The next year, at this time, Tommy is at Marine Corps boot camp, Quantico, VA, for the start of his active duty. However, based on a whistle blower complaint, NCAA investigating team arrived on campus. Told that Tommy was in the Marines, they were shocked, you mean he did not take the Peace Corps or Canada option?

Some of Tommy's experiences as a youngster that got him inspired in Sports Competition! The year the NY Giants and the Dodgers ended the season in a dead tie. As a paperboy, had his bike decorated with signs of congrats for the Dodgers! Next was Bobby Thompson, stolen signals, home run, the rest is history! Soon after, no more Ebbets Field or Polo Grounds! They got to the Left Coast first! Giants were across from the Double Play Saloon! At Seals Stadium.

Next with Giants Semi-Pro baseball. Tommy's school wanted him to play with the South Orange Giants at Cameron Field. Did it for three summers, when it was over, in silent protest against the Giants, did not take a uniform, remember these were the real NY Giant MLB flannel uniforms! During the week Tommy played twi-light ball with the Newark Red Wings!

During the Bay to Breakers Race, two high rollers lunched at the Double Play Saloon! They discussed East Coast Ball Teams moving West. It was Branch and Joe, both with input from their mob guys back east. Discussion proceeded until two swishy types sat across from Branch. He said Joe—what the hell is this? Joe said they make good ushers for your games, and we have plenty of them here at Seals Stadium. But in LA we have the Bloods and the Crippies!—Bye-Bye Blackbird! at the Biograph—1934!

Graduation from college, then destined for active duty, as a Marine Corps Infantry Officer! Was this an interruption for him in his career as a stock broker, Congressional staffer, golfer (never played), pro athlete, draft dodger, answer—**NO**! Today one could argue the plight of the country is Liberty or Tyranny, right Mark! After a summer as a Jersey Shore Lifeguard, Seaside Heights, NJ, headed to Quantico, VA. Did not know it at the time, but this was Tommy's start for a career of Public Service.

After initial training at Camp Pendleton, CA., lock on three months, spent the three months living in a snake ranch on the beach, at San Clemente, next to Richard Nixon and Pat. They said they felt safe with us nearby. Marines, in First Bn/3rd Marines, then headed for the Far East. We made up the "Ready Force", for the US, at a time when that part of the world was unstable! And right around the corner was Vietnam!

Our first Navy trip, 21 days, was from San Diego to Yokohama, Japan and Naha, Okinawa. The Battalion sailed on the USS GENERAL W.A. MANN, 1800 Marines, no dependents.

First mission was to set up the 3rd MARDIV GUERILLA WARFARE school in northern Okinawa. Remember on the ROCK was some of the bloodiest fighting of the Pacific War! The Jap pilots, conducted frenzied Kamikaze attacks on the US ships, one of which was Tommy's Uncle, a CPO, on LST-71! We all had done 3 months of 6 days a week training in the hot and arid Camp Pendleton desert. Now was time to adjust to a wet damp climate. It was critical to keep weapons and feet dry. Why? Right down the road below Hong Kong might be our future? Vietnam!

A major training activity which was required for survival in the jungle was that of employing ambush techniques. Squad leader, E-5, (13 Marines), set up on the high ground along the enemy trail. All must remain absolutely silent with safeties unlocked. On the other side we planted sharpened bamboo sticks with feces on tips. The ones that were not killed by our shooting, were pierced by the bamboo. Yes, war is HELL, but if **you don't kill them—then it is your turn! Just ask BLACKIE!**

Next, major Division size operation in Mindoro Philippines after a Mt. Fuji, Japan, live fire in November, 1/3 traveled to Mindoro on APA, LST, CVA and back to the ROCK, blasted by a Pacific Typhoon. Troops sea sick all over the place, waves crashing over deck, washed off up chuck.

Back on the ROCK, Okinawa, word came down some of us may get a trip to the Cuban Missile Crisis! Yes, made that list initially. Probably due to skill in the limbo! Looked forward to showing those Cuban Hooters, some of my Jersey Shore moves. But, wiser higher up Marine handlers said Clark go to NAD, McAlester, OK—named for House Speaker Carl Albert.

Assigned as Guard Officer for 150 Man Marine Detachment, base was a Top Secret, Navy Nuke Base, Tommy continued to enjoy the job challenge, contribution and service to the USA, and not being a "dodger". My CO, Major Robert F. Maiden, a decorated veteran of Iwo Jima, he went back to school and got commissioned. One day the local FBI Agent called him and said informants told him, workers are stealing from the base big time! We set up a sting, busted ten workers. **Semper Fi!**

Next time Tommy saw the FBI Agent, he said I notice you have baseball and basketball teams. Can I jump in for some workouts? Sure, just don't bring any lefties who also think they are basketball players or golfers! And do vacations at Martha's place.

Later, the Bureau guy said what are you doing after the Corps? Once a Marine always a Marine, was my answer,

Semper Fi! Within the year, left the Corps when time was up, did some sub-teaching during the day and worked nights on the Newark, NJ docks, based on Dad's contacts, with Tommy's high school mob buddies. After an extensive background investigation, Tommy was told to report to WDC and Quantico, VA. for training. So Tommy again headed to his second home, Quantico, Virginia now FBI.

The FBI Academy sits on 500 acres of land off I-95, within the Quantico Marine Corps Base. Each year about 25,000 apply to be new Agents and fewer than a thousand are accepted. Then it is a 20 week program to become Special Agents—FBI. Tommy finished training and was sworn in by J. Edgar Hoover, who was one of his Dad's hero's.

The ceremony was in main Justice, WDC, in the 5th floor conference room. The room had been used in 1942 to try 8 Nazi saboteurs. Six were executed at the WDC Jail and buried in Anacostia. Today the Nationals run over their graves!

J. Edgar ran the FBI for forty-eight years. Never again would one man dominate the FBI. When created on June 29, 1908, it had 34 Special Agents in DOJ. Congress was leery of a national police force, so no weapons were carried until the Dilinger era!

Looked forward to seeing Major Spooner, at Globe & Laurel, and hearing more of his stories. The Major has an outstanding book, **The Spirit of Semper Fidelis**—"Reflections from the bottom of an old canteen cup". Tommy first met the Major with Brooklyn Louie and Joe Horne.

Tommy carried his All-Star baseball talent to the Far East, playing on the Navy team at Jose Rizal Memorial Stadium in the Philippines, threw 2 complete games—Won—they wanted me to switch to the Navy, you know the answer, once a Marine, always a Marine! At the stadium, on the outfield wall were painted signs showing where Babe Ruth and Lou Gehrig had homered during a barnstorming visit for the troops.

Also, Tommy played on the McAlester Loafers, 7 wins. The team Captain was the local PD Sgt. The Right fielder and Center fielder, had done a total of seven years in prison, for moonshine. They made the best Choc (Choctow) beer ever. Clarence "Choctaw" Carnes was a good friend of Blackie's, on the Rock. They bottled it in used quart beer bottles, you knew you had the legit stuff if it had particles floating. Made in a bath tub by a man with a wooden leg, no beer license!

The temperature was over 100 degrees, on Sunday afternoons. Fans would watch from their cars with the air conditioner running, with gas prices today, not sure what they do! You can get it today at Pete's Place, Krebs, OK. Mickey Mantle's main stop on his way home! He lived in Commerce, OK. His Dad and Grandfather were zinc miners, # 7, was the best switch hitter ever! After a night on the town, batting the next day, he would claim he hit the ball in the middle!

One of the nicest guys Tommy met in OK, was a fella from Broken Bow, OK. the best lefty pitcher ever, Warren Spahn, Most Wins of any Lefty in History of Game! He ate at Pete's Place like the Mick. It was Italian with the best food! The Italians were the original residents, where they worked the coal mines.

Mick and Warren often said that Spring training was the best time in Florida. Back in OK, not good cause it was Tornado Alley! They knew many who were affected over the years. Tommy was not quite the Warren Spahn lefty, but one who hoped to make the Show. Tommy had a tryout for the Red Sox at Jersey City. Scouts had spotted him in relief at the Hall (Seton). They liked his "live" arm and lefty, thank you Sister Miriam. Best they had was "C" ball and make it on your own. Said you could sign up for the Peace Corps, be a no show—play for the Sox. Preacher Roe made it, as well as Koufax!

Soon after getting Hoffa put away, and Dr. Spock and his draft dodgers addressed, the March on the Pentagon happened. Tommy removed protesters from a flat bed truck which was sap aided (not authorized), got a Vietnam flag as a training aid. The 82nd Airborne was outstanding, in their restraint but firmness. The protesters threw burning boards at the troops, and then poured urine on them! How did they hold back?

The local paper announced the 55 years and over, baseball tryout at Central Park. At this point, Tommy had recently started training for the Alcatraz and Gate swims. But, knowing that ball got him to where he was today, he signed up. Day of try out, went to drug store to get Ben gay to apply. Came back to car and battery dead, the man upstairs was talking! No one at home, for second car rescue, Tommy walked five miles home and got car # 2, cellphones had not been invented. Off to the field, close to start time! Cost $100, get it back if don't make team.

Tommy's outfit was—Brooklyn Dodger hat, Dallas Cowboy shirt, sweats, patten leather baseball shoes—his son sent them up from Santa Barbara, he wore them when he played there! Tommy's plan was to be a BP Pitcher! With his outfit, they said you look like you are ready for the Show! So on mound, catcher comes out who is about 25 yrs junior, signals?, Well I am former FBI, so we have to keep them secret so . . . ! Outside and inside, if we get a guy that looks like he can hit, we will bean him!

First guy bats from the right, we keep it out side, Tommy is a lefty, he grounds to first, out. Next is a lefty who looks like a weight lifter, decide to do a Newark brush back, he rolls off to the right gives me a bad look as he gets up, but he knows that I may have many years on him, I am still the boss, I am the one throwing the bold ball!

He lines the next pitch to second, two outs! Next guy looks like a bunter! So the way I start, is a fast one at his head! Somehow he gets his bat up to foul it off and the catcher grabs it behind the plate near the screen! As we jog off, applause and way to go old man! If you ever have been a competitive athlete, and not a dodger, the erotic feeling was great!

With the D-1 Big East deal as a result of the Ebbets Field Dodger tryout. His dad, a Newark, NJ, Fire Captain was pleased, good example for his 4 younger brothers! They lived in the Ironbound section of Newark, wrong side of the tracks, the 5 boys shared a bedroom on the second floor, next to Club 87, a bar with Polka weddings on weekends! Like Tommy, three of the brothers became Marine Corps Officers and all served in Far East during the Vietnam Era. The youngest brother serves as a Captain in the NJ State Fire Service Department. Tommy and brothers were the first of the extended family to attend college.

BLACKIE FLASHBACK

In the 1950's, Blackie was in federal custody at Atlanta (1956-1959), for hijacking and armed robbery. He volunteered for the CIA MK-ULTRA program to research mind control drugs, headed by a CIA chemist, including LSD, to lessen his sentence. His work with CIA was used as a basis for his later assignment to Homeland on West Coast while on lam from Boston, FBI, since Dec. '95.

He got popped for passing hacksaw blades to a fellow con for an escape attempt, got first trip to left coast, to ROCK (Alcatraz), #AZ1428 Later, on lam he would return with Carol, Dec 21, 2007. He befriended Clarence Carnes, the "Choctaw Kid", on the ROCK. Carnes told BLACKIE he hoped to be buried on Indian land. Instead when he died, he was buried in a paupers grave in Missouri. When BLACKIE heard about it, he paid to have him relocated to the state where Tommy served as as a Marine Guard Officer—Oklahoma. After ROCK, it was Leavenworth and Lewis burg then back to ravage Boston as an FBI informant, and Drug Kingpin.

Tommy was in his normal window seat at the B V, when we arrived. He had hooked up with the good looking blonde staffer from WDC, and was regaling her about his swims and his Marine Corps and Law Enforcement background. We laid back, not wanting to throw a curve ball as he was delivering one strike after another! Her big blue eyes were eating—him up! Reminded Tommy that our meeting was still set for around 1500 with her boss from WDC, at Lefty O'Douls, or The Ramp! Tommy gave Blondie a big hug and kiss, and told her he would call her around 1800.

PHOTO CREDITS

Vince Rios
Map
Tiernan
Butler
Gasko
O'Brien
Kelley
Laso
Pitchess
Mueller III
Tiernan
Winstead
Law Enforcement
Freeh
Troops
WTC

Not as Lean...

Not as Mean...

but still a Marine!

Semper Fi

United States
Department of Justice

SPECIAL ACHIEVEMENT AWARD

Presented to

M. Thomas Clark

in appreciation and recognition of Sustained Superior Performance of Duty.

John N. Mitchell

Attorney General

April 6, 1971

Overall Event Counts (Boston Residents)

Overall Substance Abuse	2000	2001	2002	2003	2004	2005	2006	2007	2008	2009	2010
Treatment Admissions	NA	19,806	20,784	17,265	16,607	16,973	16,987	17,604	17,151	17,433	16,728
Helpline Calls	NA	5,202	4,540	4,247	4,217	3,409	3,253	2,348	2,801	2,647	1,790
Emergency Department Visits*	NA	NA	12,822	13,898	13,333	13,509	13,710	13,853	14,545	16,444	NA
Hospital Admissions*	NA	NA	8,276	8,806	8,741	8,702	8,557	9,018	8,102	8,161	NA
Mortality (Deaths)	134	178	168	184	159	165	215	220	176	NA	NA

Heroin/Opioids	2000	2001	2002	2003	2004	2005	2006	2007	2008	2009	2010
Heroin Treatment Admissions	NA	9,393	10,356	8,718	8,784	8,628	8,611	9,432	9,368	9,756	9,406
Other Opioids Treatment Admissions	NA	902	1,060	1,037	998	1,019	1,086	1,200	1,363	1,503	1,418
Heroin Helpline Calls	NA	1,822	1,527	1,660	1,552	1,140	1,058	712	934	892	516
Other Opioids Helpline Calls	NA	607	622	600	690	508	501	352	427	457	369
Heroin/Opioids ED Visits*	NA	NA	1,936	1,885	1,681	1,702	1,526	1,424	1,649	2,034	NA
Heroin/Opioids Hospital Admissions*	NA	NA	2,030	2,275	2,148	1,908	1,834	1,824	1,693	1,739	NA
Heroin/Opioids Mortality (Deaths)	36	71	59	75	58	51	92	92	63	NA	NA

Cocaine	2000	2001	2002	2003	2004	2005	2006	2007	2008	2009	2010
Treatment Admissions	NA	6,959	7,046	5,637	5,285	5,882	6,324	6,168	5,920	5,336	4,751
Helpline Calls	NA	1,014	896	823	805	709	726	425	491	402	304
Emergency Department Visits*	NA	NA	1,223	1,122	957	1,154	1,327	1,293	1,403	1,404	NA
Hospital Admissions*	NA	NA	1,244	1,449	1,419	1,597	1,668	1,817	1,470	1,226	NA
Mortality (Deaths)	25	39	30	52	36	30	58	55	38	NA	NA

Marijuana	2000	2001	2002	2003	2004	2005	2006	2007	2008	2009	2010
Treatment Admissions	NA	3,821	3,459	2,975	2,491	2,497	2,506	2,489	2,324	2,652	2,291
Helpline Calls	NA	283	269	193	199	148	176	108	112	96	110

Alcohol	2000	2001	2002	2003	2004	2005	2006	2007	2008	2009	2010
Treatment Admissions	NA	12,747	12,990	10,363	9,426	9,579	9,778	9,495	9,035	8,856	8,388
Helpline Calls	NA	2,740	2,310	1,958	2,034	1,722	1,683	1,286	1,425	1,308	898
Emergency Department Visits*	NA	NA	8,831	9,474	8,881	9,019	9,420	9,655	10,353	11,668	NA
Hospital Admissions*	NA	NA	4,582	4,765	4,689	4,799	4,553	4,980	4,163	4,217	NA
Mortality (Deaths)	70	86	89	79	76	89	137	96	91	NA	NA

*Emergency Department Visits and Hospital Admissions data reflect a fiscal year running October through September.
Note: With the exception of substance abuse deaths, an individual may experience more than one event. All non-mortality counts reflect the total number of events – not unique individuals.
For additional counts (e.g., subgroup), please contact the Boston Public Health Commission Office of Research and Evaluation.

UNITED STATES DEPARTMENT OF JUSTICE

FEDERAL BUREAU OF INVESTIGATION

WASHINGTON, D.C. 20535

March 28, 1966

PERSONAL

Mr. M. Thomas Clark
Federal Bureau of Investigation
Washington, D. C.

Dear Mr. Clark:

     I want to commend you for your very
fine services in the investigation and apprehension
of Stephen McKenzie Cherry, the subject of a Selective Service Act case.

     You acted with alertness in recognizing
this fugitive, despite his altered appearance, and
with aggressiveness in taking him into custody.
Through your determined and persistent efforts, he
was positively identified and I want you to know that
I am appreciative.

Sincerely yours,

J. Edgar Hoover

CHAPTER II

THE ROCK
FBI KILLER

On our last trip to WDC, we were told we would hear from the House Government and Reform Committee, meeting in the Rayburn Office Building, soon. On this first trip to the Capitol, we were directed to one of the paneled meeting rooms in the basement of Rayburn building. Somewhat like the handball courts at the South End. The bar at South End Rowing Club had more class. The Fast and Furious—ATF group, just finished what may be a never ending investigation. Next up was the Inspector General for the GSA. Tommy knew GSA, he had done a tour as the Assistant IG-GSA Investigations, San Francisco. After GSA was the Secret Service.

Staffers introduced themselves and advised that our hearing was postponed, please report back at 1000 tomorrow, but call first. Tommy suggested that the team repair to the RAMP, a National Park Service lunch area, on the Potomac River, across from Reagan Airport, where they have picnic tables and pitchers of cold beer. Tommy felt this would help the team relax and prepare!

Also, this was the location when Tommy was on the 91-88 squad, that he and Chuck would park and wait for an alert call. You could make a 91 call in short order. Down 295 to VA suburbs, or over 495 around to MD. Also, up 295 to the District of Columbia with about 120 active banks. And up 295, past Reagan Airport, and over 495 to MD. Preferred bank robbery time for perps, late PM on Friday's, for weekend partying!

Not a Friday, but with my partner Brooklyn Louie, we both had a need for caffeine. This activity was banned during work hours, was in the rule book, and could result in a one way transfer to Butte! Soon thereafter, the NY Ave minister called his friend the Big Boss. Seemed his park spot was being used by a Bureau car. Next day at the Holloway House, NY Ave and 14th, in early am, the place was visited by a SWAT team of Inspectors, who had trouble making it through all the caffeine starved Agents.! Across the street was the multi level Bureau garage. Report was a new Inspector, who was a climber, saw three who were ID, all got one way tickets to New Orleans, San Antonio and Newark. None to Butte!?

So, Tommy and Brooklyn, filled out their 3 card, contact an informant, at Fife And Drum. On way back to the OPO, heading south on 14th Street, and just before corner of the famous K Street, that Ladybird had beautified with islands and trees. The lobbyists who hang out there make millions for themselves, the Congressman and the Corporations they represent! **PROBLEM!** Twenty feet from the K Street corner, Bank Robbery **"Alert"** for bank on K Street came over the radio. Brooklyn said, "Let's git 'em Tommy", as he pulled out his .357 and checked to make sure it was fully loaded! No lights or sirens, let's sneak up on them! The Bank of Washington sign was up high on the wall to the left, Tommy drove across the red brick island with Lady's trees, then up a 50 foot red brick sidewalk. All the time as he drove, wondering did he have his gun? Not to worry, grabbed his back-up gun from ankle holster. Last year he got a ticket, from a female officer, for using cel while driving! Came to a halt just before the front door. As we went in door Brooklyn, had his badge in his left hand and the .357 in his right hand and yelled, FBI, everyone hit the deck!

We will get a commendation for this bust, if we live! We were right here. Also, in the evening hours we worked Hookers, the expensive ones, in this area. More later. Tommy took the left side of the bank, where an alley, led to a rear door, pulling out his Clint Eastwood, "MAKE MY DAY" Magnum, as he quickly moved in. Yes, Tommy was Irish—Dad—but Mom was very German and she said Sig Sauer, yes! Because of Tommy's caffeine deficit, and hurry to fill out the 3 card, did he forget his gun, leave it in the bathroom a Starbucks, drop in the car trunk,?, regardless Brooklyn is a firearms expert and would protect Tommy, who he made pay for the illegal coffee.

Due to early hour, 1000, the few customers in the bank had all hit the deck as ordered, smaller targets. To the left, vaulting the counter with money bags and guns were two perps! One fired at us, Tommy dropped him with a leg shot from his ankle gun, the other perp gave up. Tommy yelled to the manager to call a bus, the perp was bleeding heavy.

The bank was to the left, little did Tommy know, as time raced forward, also to the left would be the **Boston Killer,** on the ROCK, who was **armed** vs **Tommy!** More later. The rest of the day was devoted to prep for Dr. Benjamin, and March on the Pentagon.

Speculation in, FBI KILLER ESCAPES—is from books, magazines,newspapers, plus BLACKIE'S total of 19 whack jobs (21 according to LA Times), two women in Boston he strangled to death—Debra and Deborah, for which he no longer is "BLACKIE", but now has earned the handle—"sissy"! The following captures events that Tiernan noted before "THE" vacation ended. Clearly, that he may have been assisted by the agency that hunted the convict on his 15 year vacation that a Congressional Committee said "it was one of the greatest failures in the history of federal law enforcement". Yes, Tommy was sworn in by J.Edgar, who about now was doing back flips! For those who claim he was a cross-dressing paranoid lawman, better check your nylons, the seams are crooked!

For those that support the "rogue agent" theory, they should think in terms of higher up decision makers, probably dodgers, which, will become evident as the case unfolds. If you were BLACKIE, maybe you would wire yourself for all of your contacts with the law. BLACKIE is many things. STUPID is not among them.

The agency's target was the Mafia, the Appalachian 1957 meet was for all mobs to agree to LCN rules. Remember, before the bust, the bureau said no "national crime syndicate" existed, after 50 escaped and 58 were busted, including the "cheese man", the FBI started a "top hoodlum program"! BLACKIE returns from the Rock, to Boston, after serving three years on the ROCK, as part of a 10 year bank robbery conviction. He then fits right in to the program as a TEI. After a time, he was recruited by an agency Irishman, to help exterminate the New England Italian mob!

One of the attendees at the Appalachian meeting was Gerado "Jerry" from South Orange, NJ, the home of Seton Hall, where he lived with his wife and daughters. Tommy was a close friend of Pete, who was a AAU swimmer at the Newark AC. Pete spent his summers as a lifeguard at the upscale Booton Town & Country Club. He met, and married Patty, one of the daughters. Her dad was Gerado "Jerry", who was an Underboss in the Genovese crime family. Pete called Tommy and asked if he would be his best man. Tommy opined that he was willing, but was sure the Father-in- law, would not want a Bureau guy in the family, so to speak!

Pete offered that Jerry could get it cleared with my big boss through one of the NJ pols. Tommy never heard, but soon thereafter he got transfer orders to a special detail at the BN office.

An office was very active in the LCN area. Recently they had bugged a Mafia induction ceremony. The tip came from a TacOps guy in the BN office. The event by the Patrick crime family took place in a house in Medford, MA. The BN office bugged the induction of four men under the direction of the boss based in Rhode Island. The oath included drawing blood from the trigger finger of the four. Punishment for violation of omerta is death! The tapes brought jail time for all 15 participants!

The following are some of the recollections by Tommy Tiernan re Alcatraz, BLACKIE, Carol, the agency, etc. These were reported to authorities, and are under review. Informants are not clear on who planned the BLACKIE vacation scheme, but not worth an OSCAR—15 years—all around world, still had $850k, about 100 guns, certainly her Grey Goose Vodka needs put a hole in his savings.

In the summer of 2007, Tommy's brother needed help repairing an old barn on his property in the Santa Barbara, CA area. Tommy stayed at the Fess Parker resort, no room at his brothers place. At Parker's place, good pool, Precor cardio workout equipment, snack bar at pool, Pacific Ocean, across the street. And, you might see Daniel Boone in his coon skin cap, with Malibu!

Late spring on the ROCK, had the local FBI ERT team. Also along was the pub affairs clerk. Suggested to him that with the number of tourists, a Top Ten Poster might pay off. He looked at Tommy and said nothing? This was about 6 months before the RAT showed up. NO, it was not coincidental, they all knew, we will not get the truth until the trial or a whistle blower, comes forth. This whole thing blows Tommy away not that it was done, but the non-professional way it was handled. Snipers?

One day, while at the workout room, Tiernan spotted a white male who looked like BLACKIE, clean shaven, blue eyes, height 5'-8", he had a white towel wrapped around his hand like he had something in it, **gun-knife!** White male sensed Tommy was focusing on him, and chose to abruptly leave the workout room. Tommy tried to follow him in the hope of getting a room number to do some follow-up. NO LUCK! At the same time of sighting Blackie, there were reports by FBI from Europe and around the world! Agents said based on sightings they went to Munich, Germany, then on to

Taormina, Italy. Then Florida came into play, Disney World, Miami, Clearwater, Jacksonville, Kissimmee, and Daytona.

Daytona Beach was familiar to Tommy. His first office was Jacksonville, en route from Quantico, VA., driving through heavy rain in Georgia, radio reports stated two trains had been blown up in north Florida. Also reported was that the President was to address the Hoffa Teamster convention in Miami that weekend. Tommy drove his VW Beetle, he had purchased on Okinawa, while stationed there in the Marines.

So on leap year, Friday morning, Tommy reports to Jacksonville. Greeted by his new boss, told quickly what happened as he drove through Georgia, and that the Bureau had designated the bombings as a **"Bureau Special"**, Agents from offices up and down the coast were directed to report to Daytona Beach, **NOW!**

All Jacksonville agents were detailed to Daytona Beach, so none left in Jacksonville but Tommy, his boss and DK. Not unlike when he was an Infantry Platoon Commander in Corps. Usually you get an orientation at a new office, but here was the situation, ASAC pointed to map, Bu cars here, this is shopping center that just had a bank robbery, you are the Agent-In-Charge, no other agents there, **don't embarrass the bureau**! Worked the case until the wee hours with the locals, who I never met before, in the dark some shots were fired, but no one hurt, no holes in the Bureau car! **No Butte!**

So, first day of about 20 hours straight work. Great kick off for Tommy's VOT! More later. Next day, they had him in equipment car carrying stuff to Daytona, not like the Corps where we had all the emergency gear was ready to go. It being the weekend the bureau relaxation started at about 1800 on the beach. Got a chance to meet his new office Agents, collectively they said who are you, we saw you on the TV news about the Bank job this week and when they said you were bureau, who the hell is he? Well welcome, another Marine! We had more bombings, when an informant, not BLACKIE, assisted us in the bust. When the trains blew up, it was 55 box cars all over the country side, no one hurt. Someone got to Hoffa later on, but this was early in his career. Tommy sort of knew Jimmy, had worked on his jury tampering case in WDC, before Jacksonville, Florida. Through first month in first assignment, no draft dodgers. **Semper Fi!**

BLACKIE FLASHBACK

On Wednesday, August 8, 2007, **James William Lawlor, DEAD,** Natural/unnatural causes?, probably smothered to death with a pillow by BLACKIE—Carol #20. This done after he got ID from the person he saw on the bench? BLACKIE said he was illegal and used the **Lawlor** ID for doctors, NOTE—BLACKIE has a serious heart condition that is dependent on Atenolol (50 MG), according to Law Enforcement he went to Mexico to buy it, drive a car, and open a bank account. ALSO, the betting in the at Bureau was, his life expectancy will grow shorter! and shorter—**WRONG!**

All this, while never in Europe, but in Santa Monica, CA and Grey Goose cocktails at Marshals! A final shot is to check with coroner re Lawlor, and bullet holes from BLACKIE'S 100 guns—?, if they were really his! It was about this time, that the US Marshalls Service joined the hunt for Blackie? They are still looking for Frank Lee Morris and the Anglin brothers, from the famous Alcatraz Escape, June 11, 1962, all on overtime with Marshal Dillion, Chuck Connors, and Dirty Harry! Remember, Blackie was on the ROCK till it closed in March of 1963, maybe he assisted Morris and the Anglin brothers in their escape, June 11, 1962? And, you left coast staff, know the SF Office display has a post card to the ROCK Warden, saying thanks for all his help from South America?

As a reward to themselves for whacking old man Lawlor for his Identification, Carol suggested a road trip. She was getting stir crazy, and well on her way to becoming a Grey Goose Alcoholic! Without telling BLACKIE, she silently called him **"IRA"** (Irish Rat Asshole) he often got very nasty with his screaming? So, IRA says ok, let's take a road trip up US 1 to the ROCK, so I can check on my old crib, with stops along the way. He grabbed a small athletic bag, put in about a half-dozen hand guns and ammo. On his person was a Sig Sauer P226, 9mm, auto, night sights and a Glock 27 Auto. Also, had his trusty knife, a Gurkha Army knife called the Khukuri. For more info on weapons, google it!

BLACKIE said we will stay at the Hilton, Universal City, and from there we can do the Warner Brothers VIP Studio Tour, and then get some Lucchese boots at the Country General Store in Van Nuys, CA, on way to horseback riding in Hollywood with Roy Rogers. Next day we do the TMZ tour as we leave for Santa Barbara, Fess Parker Resort.

BLACKIE liked the Warner Tour, especially the treatment for "Departed" with Jack Nicholson playing **BLACKIE**. The boots and horse ride was great, always wanted Lucchese boots. He got an Enterprise rental at the Hilton, full size Ford, Crown Vic, black, cop car! It was an hour and a half to Fess Parker's place. After all, knew it well, it was home away from home! Over the past 15 years they had been there often. **BLACKIE**

liked the Precor cardio equipment and the overall privacy. It was the same as the Grand Luxxe II, Brio Gimnasio Fitness Center, workout facility that they frequented on the numerous road trips to Puerto Vallarta, Mexico, during his 15 year vacation. The Precor cardio equipment was brand new and numerous, for his daily workouts. Probably, he stuck with a daily workout based on doctor's advice re his heart condition. With what this guy did to other humans, it is hard to imagine he had a "heart"! Carol was a golfer, and did the Jack Nicklaus Academy of Golf, while Blackie did cardio!

So, they bounced between Fess Parker's in Santa Barbara, CA and the Grand Luxxe II, in Puerto Vallarta, Mexico. At BRIO GIMNASIO—Gran LUXXE, Blackie worked out daily. Between 0900 and 1300, while Carol did the Jack Nickelus Academy of Golf, and the links on alternate days. BLACKIE worked very hard, according to his trainer, RAFAEL: YOGA, Spinning, Zumba, Pilates, Stretching, and Abs, every day. It is no wonder why he was in such great shape! Carol usually hit the Grand Luxxe bar around noon every day to make sure the Grey Goose Vodka was OK! Jairo was her regular bartender, and he said most days she really put them away! Question? Who was the handler who made the reservations, was it paid on bureau credit cards, for all of his TEI travel for 15 years? By now we know all this European travel was a crock of bullshit, and the alleged travel by Agents to the European sites qualifies as questionable? The Committee needs to probe.

Back in Santa Barbara, CA, after LA, and to depart in the morning for ROCK. That night it was a toss up between the Enterprise Fish Co. and the Paradise Cafe which serves the best burgers in town, nice outdoors. BLACKIE wanted burgers, she said as long as they have Grey Goose Vodka, I am in!

They left first thing the next day cause they wanted to get to Cambria. The Hearst Castle was Wednesday by noon. Stayed at the Fog Catcher Inn, right on the ocean. The Castle was great and crowded, took him 15 years to build, on top of the hill. Run by CA parks personnel. More freedom to roam on castle grounds, because of pay cuts. Then to the Moonstone Bar and Grill, a short way down the road. Outdoors, great view of the Pacific sunset!

Carmel Valley Ranch, purchased by Clint, GOP Convention Speaker, to "chair". Modern type layout, lodge,with cabins spread all over. They planned to get to the ROCK by noon on Friday. Already the weather was colder with the fog covering the area. Carol said "too cold", Blackie said "shut up", drink some more of your Grey Goose shit, you put in the trunk with my guns!

Tommy's work day usually was Friday and he got up early. Back in boot camp days, it was 0500, on the street, showered and shaved, not like the routine for the dodgers! Out the door, to beat heavy traffic, on the route south. At pier 32-34, the America's Cup, five Cats were being hoisted into the Bay. They all had sails that reached to heaven. Right then he concluded, would rather see the old boats even if they were slower! Told Jersey Shore relative that the new Cats were not as desirable as the old boat. A few weeks later, one of the Cats flipped over in the San Francisco Bay and a crewman was killed! The city is building up the pier 32-34 area, for a Warrior Basketball Arena, which in an earthquake, will sink, or float back to Oakland!

Last year, Tommy got a call from the Warriors, asking would he like to be the Director of Security. Position requires travel to all games, deal with players and staff, and the cheerleaders! Told them PI workload was too heavy now, call next year. Tommy stopped at Red's Java House, on 32 for Java, of course! Month before gave Sean, the owner, a Top Ten Poster of Blackie, that he posted at Red's.

Here comes winter, Dec. 21, 2007, the Friday before Christmas, an exceedingly cold and foggy day, which often happens this time of year. Due to the holidays, Rangers were at a minimum for the day, many taking advantage of year end vacation days.

At around 1400, Tommy agreed to help a lady and her son, who was about 14 years old, in a wheel chair with withered legs! She said they had tried other Rangers earlier but they were too busy with school groups that had reservations. She said their time was short, because they had a flight from SFO at 1800. She said her son wanted to see the Bird man's cage (cell). She said he had done a lot of reading about the ROCK!

One look at this youngster with withered legs, **spina bifida**, in a wheelchair, and Tommy wanted to bring the Bird man back in person, so this kid could talk to him! Little did Tommy know that within the hour, Tommy would see, the **BOSTON KILLER**! Again, they wanted to see, Stroud's cell which is located off limits on the 2nd floor, about mid-way down hall, above the mess hall. The cell was the HQ for the Marines in the movie, "THE ROCK",—1996, with Sean **Connery,** Nicolas **Cage** and Ed **Harris.** We needed an elevator, Tommy being new, could not recall whether it was working.

He decided to check, with the office and the Ranger in charge. Returning to the boy and his Mom, Tommy passed behind the four theaters that show the "Alcatraz" history, a continuos movie, from Discovery that runs for 20 minutes. Then its a right at the bookstore, down the narrow passageway to the main outside path, to the boy and his Mom.

Tommy's main talk each day is about **"ALCATRAZ ESCAPES"**. He gave it from 1100 to 1200. He had a crowd of over 100. The talk started at the dock, then moved to the old burnt out (Indian Occupation) Army Officers Club, that was later used as a Rec Club by the Guards—two bowling Alleys. From this location Tommy pointed out the Morris—Anglins escape route: cell bloc roof, down bakery pipe, down path under the Water tower, to Bay behind Power Building, then?? did some one pick them up, was it an Ebb tide pick up and to China, OR were they a Great White dinner,? The Bureau was there the next AM with the dogs, should have had them there when Tommy called on Dec. 21, 2007.

Also included, he told of other major escape attempts and Tommy showed them both Wanted Posters for BLACKIE and Carol, reward for $2 M. Blackie did 3yrs. for BR, on the ROCK the most time he spent in any of his Fed homes. Next was Leavenworth, and Lewis burg, before returning to Boston to run the Winter Hill Gang. Upon his return, after about a year, he became very friendly with one of his old Irish school buddies, who was an FBI Agent!

Remember, the actual TOP TEN WANTED POSTERS for BLACKIE and Carol, were shown by TOMMY. The tourists also saw the 5 missing cons pictures: Frank Lee Morris, Anglin brothers—June 1962, Ted Cole and Ralph Roe December 1937. Also displayed was a chart of factors why it was impossible to escape—

1. **Cold Bay**—55 degrees year around—hypothermia?

2. **Distance**—about 2 miles to SF and three and a half to Angel Island.

3. **Currents**—swirling both flood and ebb tides!

4. **Great Whites**—they party at Farallones Islands, come in Bay for desert!

Tommy then tells the tourists, back in the day, he swam the Golden Gate North and the next year he did it South, passing kidney stones. Also, did Alcatraz to SF, twice. Did swims age 55 and 55 degrees in Bay, strong currents, about 2miles, no wet suit, Great Whites? Tourists ask why do it? Are you nuts? I am a MARINE we love Challenges! And Yes I am Irish—not too smart!? Also a D-1 student-athlete, baseball, after a tryout for Brooklyn Dodgers at Ebbets Field, and Captain—MVP of Swim Team, at Big East Hall! Seton Hall, Atlantic Ocean Lifeguard, Seaside Heights, N J. Where Snookie made her Olympic debut!, Jersey Shore, before MARINES!

The swims based on bet with Marine buddy for Jameson's and Black BUSH at the iconic Buena VISTA! Swim day, Tommy gets ride in T-Bird to South End Rowing Club Swim Coaches. Bob the Sheriff and Randy, world renowned attorney for his defense of George Farnesworthy - 17 arrests (for pimping at Cow Palace bar) - no convictions! En route they remind Tommy the South Gate is the toughest of the Swims, Ebb tide, that in later years caused a fatality in the America's Cup Race's, that the ORACLE won! Also, oil tankers move through the Bay on a time schedule, with hungover Irish Captains. Yes, swim hard, your titanium replaced shoulder may be rusting out and won't last much longer! Also, add to the list

Great Whites, Earthquakes and JUMPERS - depressed cause they could not get obama care coverage. If your Speedo's slip off because in your haste you forgot to tie them, then the Irish Coffee at the Buena Vista will really taste good!

The TOP TEN POSTER reminded him of another when he was assigned to Florida. They had finished a hard week on the train bombing case, around 1900 all of Squad 2, got a call back to the office. No happy hour, Jack Clauuser, former Florida cop, slipped out of the nut house, consider **A & D**! He was an ITSMV perp who chose to write the Director and tell him he was a jerk, because his guys could not catch him! Known as the **Florida Fox**, who ever got him would get a special reward, not Butte! Tommy, new kid on the block, was assigned to Roy from OK. After briefing, Roy, who was Tommy's training Agent, said get a car, bring it around to the front and I will meet you their with the shotguns. It began to rain, the hurricane was to the North of GA, but still had a bunch of rain for us. We had a monsoon, like the Japan typhoon, had hotels on the strip, with his photo to check. Next day Roy asked how did we do. Told him I busted the perp stuffed him in trunk, said they could call the Director, get the credit, Roy, just hope he does not give you BUTTE!

Tommy, Roy said I am sorry about last night, but I already had two good screwdrivers when they called. Needed the OJ for my diabetic shit! Some how the **Fox** gets to the Left Coast. Arrested by SFPD for attempted rape in a flop house on Market Street. Not clear whether he was after a male or a female, I will leave that to you SF experts. No more letters to the Director. Before his SF bust he was questioned, asked to take off his shirt, he refused, they let him go. They were instructed, next time you draw down on the subject, say—"Make My

Day", and finish your inspection for scars and tattoos with your Magnum pressing the temple, loaded of course!

BLACKIE FLASHBACK—

Blackie soon became a Top Echelon Informant for the agency, at the same time he built business activity in narcotics distribution which probably resulted in lives ruined for young Boston human beings. Greater than the number he is charged with whacking and/or his pedophile type victims, extortion, money laundering, conspiracy to commit murder, and possibly 19 whack jobs, plus, all worth $50 million.

On the "Escapes" tour Tommy told the tourists to print from the internet the pictures, so we could share the $ 2M! Tommy was asked often why the "BLACKIE" poster only had full face frontals and no profiles and was last printed July 7, 2007. Tourists comments, "maybe they were not interested in capturing him"?—15 years? This comment made me think, an extremely attractive young brunette with a knockout body, blue eyes, a Philippine Marine LT., Roxy, who insisted she was a secret agent, took me to the Buena Vista, a pub up the street, from the South End. We did it at the end of my tour, she shared with me her dark deep secret on input from some Homeland sources. First we checked the table, top and bottom, for sound devices, why. This place was often visited by 1811's and the IA guys, who were known to OD on Irish Coffee! We then adjourned to the SERC, for a night tour conducted by Bob the Sheriff, and Randy!

The pictures with the glasses are exactly the same except for the mustache, taken in 2000 in Fountain Valley, CA.? Also, no female tourists ever said they were from Iceland. At the time, the fugitives were residents of Santa Monica, since April 1998, on property records, see the, 10 page, FD-302, Sallie—Stephanie, October 9, 2011, "Whitey in exile," only a short 5 hour drive from his former home on the ROCK! Tommy's 45 years in Law Enforcement told him someday the RAT, will be back to visit and see if they took care of his crib ('59 to March 21, 1963), when AG Kennedy closed the ROCK March 21, 1963.—it is a long way from all the exotic European locations where the agency claimed he was sighted.

BLACKIE FLASHBACK

On December 21, 2007, he's BACK! First, left Carol by the Alcatraz theater, too damn cold for her bones, even though she had been fortified with Grey Goose Vodka. Blackie went topside to check his "crib" and see if any changes were made. Later when Blackie saw the solar panels being installed on the cell bloc roof, he knew the seagulls protest was to continue to make their deposits—resulting in ineffective solar. The water tower was getting fixed, all cell doors were fixed, and it was indicated this was in preparation for the transfer of the Guantanamo prisoners to the ROCK, an Administration and Congress decision. Of course, the work was made possible by use of Stimulus Funds! And, sales of the House and Senate buttons.

Tommy returned toward the boy and his Mom. On the way down the passage, a white male came around the corner from outside, probably back from the cell block above, appeared to hesitate—when he saw Tommy, like he was going to retreat back! Yes, in fatigues Tommy looked like a cop. But, when you have the best law agency in the world, on your side, and you have a knife and a machine pistol under your big topcoat, worst case you blow Guides head off, just above his Marine Corps pin. So he continued toward Tommy, probably because he told Carol he would be back, and did not want the Grey Goose Vodka Lady "screaming" at at him, knowing she had many V juices to warm up. It has been a long time since his fugitive and BR work, on the street.

WHAT—as Tommy's street juices that had been dormant since he left 45 years at DOJ, he was close to bashing IRA into the concrete wall, but the bump under his coat—NO! No metal detectors on the island, like when the prison was operational—shives. Once you chase a perp down, it stays with you forever, like once you learn how to play the right field wall at Ebbets, or the left field wall at Fenway, you never forget! Back to the RAT, who definitely looked like the poster convict that Tommy used in his talks, as the RAT gets closer, stomach tightens, is this really the guy that the agency said was sighted on numerous times at European locations. Shocking realization maybe, he is the **"Boston Killer"**! Some quick thoughts Tommy had—welcome him back to the ROCK and ask if liked the new paint job on his old crib; did he help Morris and the Anglin's escape and did they join him on his murders with the Winter Hill gang; would he mind double bunking with the Guantanamo prisoners or would he pull his seniority? Tommy could not risk harm to his two guests, so he planned to move on and radio ahead.

Understand, all this was happening in real time! He continued toward Tommy and the book store around the corner, hallway was very narrow. As he approaches, Tommy says," hey where are you from?", like Tommy said to all tourists. The RAT stares through Tommy and says nothing—like the Bureau guy in the summer. Now as he is closer, wishing he had his .357 Magnum! Guides not armed on Alcatraz! He looks through Tommy, corner of his mouth is curled, with clear BLUE beady eyes, cold as marbles, that drill into you, and says nothing!

He wears a white ball cap, no lettering, about 5' 7", heavy black top coat, hands in coat like he was holding a knife or a machine pistol as he passes Tommy. Looks to be late 70's, good shape, no disguise. No metal detectors on island! Tommy finally saw his left profile (not on Top Ten Wanted Poster), he passes, recalling a Boston alert that said he always carries a knife and is proud of his three year stretch on the ROCK, and that "he never will go back to prison"! Fleeting thought, get him, it is worth $2m, you are a retired Fed, so you qualify for the big "2". Later Tommy, makes a quick call back to Jersey Shore to brothers who say, The RAT would have made you "swiss cheese". As The RAT is about to pass, from behind a hoarse female voice yells "Ranger where is the bookstore?", as Blackie passes, it is Carol his blue-eyed girlfriend! More on this later.

Also, a fleeting thought, extend my hand for a shake, Welcome him back and, did we take good care of your crib? Seeing his hand I could judge better if I could take him. Tommy thought, for an Irish Marine, this was "a lot to process". But had this RAT not been "protected", this sordid chapter could have ended TODAY! Later, realized he said nothing back, not because he did not like my looks, after all, I am Irish too, not an Irish RAT, but his Boston accent would have iced him!

Probably did not want a former Irish Agent to beat his handler out of $2 M. OK, now that Tommy had time to think about what just happened. Give me a break, Tommy is sure that his time with the Marines, FBI, and DOJ-SF-IG can explain what just happened! This SOB piece of crap, had he chosen to, could have blown Tommy away, because his old outfit wanted so bad to get the mob, they sacrificed the rules they had for

Top Echelon Informants. Who did it, some people in the organization that J.Edgar made the best in the world. No, not instructional to state the names of those responsible, you know who you are, probably dodgers, it did not happen, had that piece of shit done Tommy in,—**FOUR MARINE BROS—DEATH BY STRANGULATION—Bye—Bye—Blackie—BIRD!**

Darwin Coon, BR, Tommy met on the ROCK, he wrote book how he evaded the FBI. When Tommy told him he was on the Hoover 91 squad back in the day, Darwin stared him down and spat on the ROCK deck! BLACKIE no doubt had "recorded on his wire" the exchange with Tommy, as he always did during his career in dealings with the law. What the agency did not factor in was BLACKIE'S CUNNING. His attorney requested his trial date be delayed due to the preponderance of material to be prepared and the related stress, to some time around St. Patrick's Day! **Semper Fi!**

Back in the day, for East Coast guys, the NIT and St. Patricks Day was the place to be! The NIT, before the NCAA big show, was at the Garden. Tommy was a brand new USMC Lt., the St. Patrick's Day Parade was next day. Two of Tommy's D-1 basketball guys were busted for point shaving, on eve of NIT. Daily News, his brothers paper, broke the news on the eve of the NIT. It was coach Reagan's first year, like Tommy he had been a Marine. Both players were nice guys, the one Tommy knew best had a problem, he had trouble reading! One plus was that Tommy hooked up with the Marine Buck Sgt., with the knock out body, that Bob Gerard had him guard while skinny dipping in Honolulu, they went to McSorley's til very late!

Then on St. Patrick's Day, on law enforcement business, just after 9-11, visited NY. Stayed at the NY Athletic Club, next to Central Park. Had a business meeting at Rocky Sullivan's pub on Lexington Ave. Met one of many contacts, a looker from USA, she had ducats for Tommy for Mass at St. Patrick's on the Day! We talked about BLACKIE being a homosexual and a pedophile to add to his resume as an FBI **Informant**.

Next morning to the Cathedral a good hour before service, ducats were for last year? Time to improvise, as instructed, knocked on gigantic side door, no answer. Being an altar boy, pinned my SFPD badge on my blue blazer lapel. Checked my shamrock tie headed up the steps, having never been there before, another new experience. Back in the day, Tommy was an altar boy at St. Ann's Catholic grade school, 3 blocks from his house. Around the corner is where Brooke's mother lived, married to a VP at the Ballantine's Brewery. On the cold winter mornings, Tommy fortified himself with some red, Fr. Mooseburger, left in the carafe, for the sprint home!

As Tommy enters the sacristy, he quickly moves past the two security personnel, who assume Tommy is one of them (the lapel—SFPD—badge). Off to the left is Cardinal Egan, checking his GREEN head gear. Tommy proceeds to the church, which is almost full. Tells the usher near the door he knocked on, he will handle it. He then sees a fireman in uniform, with his family—wife, 3 youngsters. He is on crutches, maybe a 9/11 victim, Tommy escorts all of them to the very front row, makes room for them! **Semper Fi**! Tommy leaves the Cathedral, for Egan's Pub, near the Plaza Hotel. Egan's serves free Irish breakfast, not his favorite **(no grits).** At the Plaza, it is the N.Y.Governor breakfast, no ticket, tell the cute girl, left it at hotel, pop my creds, she says have a good time!

Then to NYAC by noon and get car to Newark Airport for 1400 flight to WDC. So, the parade is in full swing, love parades, especially bagpipes! St Patrick's Day in NY, it seemed every other unit has pipes. Plan was to walk north on 5th Ave next to parade. Problem, sidewalk full of people. So, it was time to march in the parade! Jumped barricade, asked head guy if I could join them, said yes, but no cartwheels! Was more stuff with a good looking lady from McAlester, OK. I was a MARINE there, she worked at the Mc Alester State Prison where Mc Veigh, the Oklahoma City bomber was fried! **Semper Fi!**

BLACKIE FLASHBACK

So near the Marine Corps Birthday, November 10, Blackie meets one of his guys, Shotgun, at the Lions Statues at the New York Public Library. Tommy's grandfather was a German stone carver from the old country, he did those Lions! No doubt he did not appreciate **BLACKIE**, meeting there. Blackie meets his main man Shotgun, and sez he never will return to Boston! Prior to their meet, the NYO, TacOps, guys bugged the lions for intelligence and VOT! Blackie says to Shotgun, need to move on, there's trouble and I'm going away for awhile, but I have insurance that is gold plated! The Lions—roared very loud! He said he taped every meet, and dinners with the law for the last thirty years, and they are locked up in a law Library vault in Boston, he got a special lease price through a relative,with copies in a Cavan Bank! He said he got some new thick war books about great Generals, of course he stole them from the New York Library, please advise the Marine Police Chief Ray, if he is off the no contact list! These were added to his collection of Batman comic books, his favorite!

Blackie is indicted, tells handler he wants vacation advice from the Bureau, just like any other employe. Not going to take the fall and wanted help as a TEI Bureau guy. He proposed a vacation out of Boston to the left coast. Handler said Bureau suggests California, southern, you can hook up with our LA Office and locate in Santa Monica, CA From there you can access the coast and Mexico, our Legat can help there. We will provide you with cell phones to get us 24 hours a day. Like before, no murders while you are on lam!

BUT, remember we work closely with Homeland. They need lots of help on the West Coast going after the China spies. Ten China Air 747's arrive daily on the West Coast and the last 5 rows are set aside for spies. You will report through us to them. Take Carol with you, good cover, will advise them of your Grey Goose needs. Blackie said, remember I am a AF vet, you guys don't do service. So, if I get banged up, get me to the VA in LA. No need to dig into my $millions made from Boston drugs, etc. Too bad about the kids that either OD'd, became vegetables, or committed suicide, their choice! Next time, will buy a funeral pantheon, and after Lee Morris, the Anglins, John and Clarence, whack'em, easier to dump!

So until December 21, 2007, he was reported to be all over the world, BUT now we know that was a pile of crap! Someday we will know the truth, meantime at the Bureau, the Chaplin directs weekly novenas, that the RAT has an event like his 19 plus—Soon!

Meanwhile back on the ROCK, Blackie is up in cell block checking his old crib. Carol did not go to see his crib, did not give a shit! Too cold, she was really getting homesick, and on her way to being a Grey Goose Alcoholic, about to lose her liver on the deck.

As **Blackie** passes Tommy, to Tommy's left rear up the passage way, a strong husky female voice, up to the left, near the Book Store yells, "Hey Ranger where is the book store"?

Clearly this was to distract Tommy so she could protect **Blackie.** Tommy turns to see a blond in, powder blue ski outfit and cap, blue eyes, about 5' 7", she was a "dead ringer" for her poster photo, neither attempted to wear a disguise on ROCK. Yes, these two were talked about in a recent Sunday Talkie.

Made one wonder if this and other trips were done with a Bureau escort? Her prominent "red nose", the cold weather and probably Grey Goose Vodka cocktails, to ward off the the cold weather!. Carol was well dressed for the very cold and coming from Santa Monica, CA., where it is warmer, they purchased WalMart clothes for trip? Her height was about the same as **Blackie,** she was about 5'-7", no disguise. Why do a disguise if you are being protected by the best law agency in the world!

When they dined frequently at Michael's, in Santa Monica, CA, the waiter said they paid about $200 in cash, for meal and had Grey Goose Vodka Cocktails topped off by wine.! They sat at table 23, in the corner of the outdoor courtyard. Who knows but the handlers, concerned they may do something stupid, got a limo and drove them up to the ROCK, and back to Santa Monica, CA. Check the office charges for December 2007, or the monthly mileage on the office limos.

Dealing with the two sightings was over quickly, radioed an alert to office, but radio transmission was broken, which happened often with the old radio's. So off we went to the Bird man's cell, to fulfill the request of the boy with no legs, up on the 2nd deck. Yes, as I told the kid and his Mom about the Bird Man (not Burt Lancaster), who had murdered a man in Alaska sentenced to McNeil Island, WA, then to Leavenworth where he stabbed to death a guard in front of 1200 inmates at lunch. The Director of the Federal Prison system then moved Stroud to Alcatraz.

On to Alcatraz where he finished his 50 years in Federal prison, "no birds"! Stroud wanted his Leavenworth birds, Warden said no! When he first got to ROCK, he was assigned to D Block (bad boys). After an evening meal The Bird man (Robert Stroud), incites a riot! Finally the guards shut out the lights. Next morning, they found all cells thrashed except for, you guessed it, Robert Stroud's—perfectly neat/clean.

So he then is moved to the Medical Unit cell, three times bigger then his previous one, two beds, one to sleep, other for a desk! Crazy like a fox! Stroud died one day before JFK, Springfield, MO,Fed Prison. On that date, Tommy at Quantico in FBI Boot Camp, NAC #8, time before was with Marines, Basic School 5-60!

In retrospect, Tommy should have had the Mom take on Blackie, she was a certified black belt and owned a Martial Arts studio in Freeland, WA. Tommy could have handled "red nose", Grey Goose Vodka! Also, Tommy thought about a reward cut for the Mom and kid, cause had they not come along then, he would have completely missed the Top Ten Rat!

Tommy was still working through the two in his mind. While on the street, in a major office on the East Coast, working fugitives and 91's, Tommy had lead on a perp at Dupont Circle. Perp was disguised, Tommy got a reward, $150, and a letter of commendation from the Big Boss! Here is the Back Story. . . .

Who was my partner that day? You got it, Brooklyn Louie. Showed Louie the photo. He said, so what? Told him my informant puts him at Dupont Circle, once and while. MD has him as lead suspect in two rapes, and we have him in DC as a draft dodger! Louie said he looks like a queer! OK, so he is a queer, rapist, draft dodger! He is no different than most citizens, but he should be busted. Louie looked out the 5th floor window of the OPO, and noted a slight drizzle. He opined he does not work in foul weather, especially with queers. Then I swung him to my side, Louie, the guy at the Dupont Circle has the greatest Nathan's dogs with mustard and kraut—like Coney Island. The perp is over 6', around 195 lbs. and a 2" scar in center of his fore head, A&D. Louie said what time do we leave?

We parked the car in spot covered by trees. The drizzle had just about stopped, got our dogs, Tommy paid, about 75 feet across the park was a fountain area, males talking. Soon one of them begins to leave, sort of toward us cause that is the path, grass wet from Louie's drizzle. As Tommy gets a better look, sez that is the asshole! With that we both adjust our cuffs and guns, not sure what the rest might do as they see the bust go down, it is a drug hang out!

Tommy moves in behind the suspect, who wears a Mexican type jacket that could hide knife or weapon. Tommy calls "Steve Cherry", figuring he will turn around. Does not, so Tommy catches up, shows his creds and asks for his name? He says Steve Wilson. Where are you from, he says Brooklyn. With that, Brooklyn Louie asks him about Brooklyn, perp can't answer, AND Tommy brushes the hair on his forehead back, and there is the 2" scar! So on the deck, cuffed and back to OPO. He still refuses to give his name, says we are harassing him! He still refuses to say who he is, as we photo and print him, supervisor comes by after looking at the perp, says to Tommy, he is the wrong guy, I am relief today and unless we have a miracle we both get Butte! Prints came back, "it's him"!

No Butte, just hot and humid D.C. **Semper Fi**! The prints were fast, in old days it was around block from OPO, not to WVA. And this guy was a real "draft dodger", and maybe a rapist!

BLACKIE FLASHBACK—

OK—Right then Tommy had decided to get a second opinion and called one of his four law enforcement brothers on the East Coast, told 'em the whole story. They said you may have missed the $2 million, BUT you would have looked like "swiss cheese", had you tried to take him!

As Tommy said goodbye to the Bird man group, he refocused on the convicts. **RESULTS**—No photo surveillance on Pier #33, where tickets are purchased for the 15" boat ride to the Island Prison. They run all day, every half hour or 1.5 mil people a year. The island had no cameras at dock, at the cell block, or the big book store. No photos of the two cons located. Also, no metal detectors on island. **Swiss cheese!** Still searching the Island for the subjects, no luck. They must have used escape tunnel that John Mason used in the movie, "THE ROCK", cause they disappeared for the next three and a half years. Should check with Art Director, Edward T. and Set Decorator Rosemary, to learn about the decaying underground tunnels deep below below the ROCK. During the construction of the prison, the top 2 stories of the Citadel were removed, and prison was built over it. So the Citadel basement was retained, but off limits. So the Mason tunnel indeed could have been used by the convicts because **Blackie** would know where it was located!

Next, gave a call to the SF bureau office, told of two sightings on ROCK, said it may fit in with other leads they had working, he hurriedly said he would send it up the line! The clerk sounded like he was hurried, maybe getting ready to attend the annual office Christmas Party at the Marines Memorial Club on Sutter St. Or, did I just live through a rerun of the movie "Departed".

Just before New Year's Day, Tommy gets a call from a male who refused to give his name, says he is from the BN office, says he wanted to know what happened on the ROCK. If this guy was BN, he is the only one from the outfit that put the RAT on the Top Ten who expressed interest in the sighting. It could have been BN bureau clerk, who advised being former bureau, Tommy should have called "OO", Office of Origin   Boston. Then he opined the field troops were sick and tired of this RAT RUSE, directed by HQ, because some HQ jerk made a rotten decision! He said the good Agents continue to bail out as fast as they can because of this Top Ten piece of crap, and the stupid moves by HQ for the past 30 years, concluded by hoping someone could get word to the press, IG, Congress, HQ to blow this whole thing out of the water!

"NO SHIT", had I known this was a "big ruse", I would have contacted the Marine Corps Commandant, because the chain of command until you get to the **Corps, STINKS.** Same Tommy told the Boston press lady who called, who said it could not have been Blackie who Tommy sighted because he visited the ROCK when he first went on lam, Sallie LNU, advised. BN voice was difficult to hear, like he was using one of the cel phones they gave **Blackie** (check the SIM cards).

Tommy Tiernan decided it was time to take MARINE action on the situation. Called an old friend he had helped on security for the Inaugural, who was on the staff of the House Government Oversight and Reform Committee, that is located in the Rayburn Office Building.

After hearing Tommy's summary, he briefed his boss the Chief of Staff, and he called Tommy back and said please get here ASAP. He said you should plan on flying to WDC, to give the Chief an in person briefing. This will avoid the DOJ, but still the info where it can be acted upon. It will protect you and your CA PI license #007, as to reporting fraudulent activity. It is noon Monday, time to check on plane and place to stay. Got place to stay near Theisman's in Old Town. When on job, made this trip often. The meet was at Rayburn building, Wednesday morning. Tommy last was there when he met with Sen John Glenn, Marine and Astronaut, just before he retired! SEMPER FI!

Tommy left SFO early Tuesday morning and arrived Dulles about 1500. Perfect plan to make the Marine Barracks Tuesday Evening Parade at the Marine Corps Memorial, at 1800. Jumped into his waiting Hertz Full Size Crown Vic, cop type car, and headed north on the George Washington Parkway. Did this so many times could almost do it blind folded. Showed my creds, Marine Major—snappy salute—to VIP parking. YES, the parade was OUTSTANDING, often wish I did not retire so I could continue to see the MARINES PARADE. Also, brings back memories of the NAVY YARD BANK BUST, Tommy worked back in the Day, more later! SEMPER FI!

After parade dropped by the Army—Navy O'Club and had a pop for old times sake. The young lady at the bar was pleasantly aggressive with her well toned body! Brklyn was intrigued by Tommy's Marine and FBI tours. All around the world, Alcatraz—Gate Swims, no wet suit—55° and great whites, as her big blue eyes dazzeled, saying that her place was close by . . . shared the Brooklyn Dodger story . . . ?

Next day met Chief of Staff in compartmented security space. Reported on Butler sightings on the ROCK and that the Bureau was non-responsive. At the end Chief said it was his turn. He knew all about Butler and the bureau. However, at the very highest levels, it was decided that Blackie was in the best position to assist the US, in the National Security area by working with Homeland given his USAF service! He has already been given TS briefings for 10 days. We know he has Carol with him, good cover. He will report through the bureau to Homeland! His Boston whack jobs and obliterating "Southie" youth, as he became the $50 million BN Drug Kingpin, will be addressed by the courts in due time! We will contact you on a weekly basis, and when necessary, get you back here to testify!

Blackie will help in the National Security area regarding the China Spies that are pouring into the US and stealing West Coast military secrets. Also, his background in drug trafficking can be applied along the Border Stations to interject the flow of the drugs into U.S., working with ATF, DEA, FBI, and ICE!

What does this tell you about any real interest in scooping up **Blackie**, who killed 19 human beings, including 2 women he strangled to death, and executed the kids on his drugs. Back in the old days, this lack of response, would result in a visit from Internal Affairs, putting all personnel on box, and issue a report to the Big Boss! Then 2 bureau buses would leave the Academy at Quantico at 0600, arrive in Boston at 1800, load up those who did not resign, then head non-stop, with rest, to the Butte Office.

Now the **BLOCKBUSTER**!! The only alleged CA sighting of the two fugitives was in Fountain Valley, CA, 2000. He sat in car while she got a spa treatment. Then we have Dec 21, 2007, on the ROCK. Why should they, it seems, know where he was all the time? Tommy personally dealt with this issue from December 21, 2007, until the HOLLYWOOD OSCAR DIRECTED type bust on June 22, 2011, in Santa Monica, CA. The earliest reported and reputable sighting was by Tommy on the ROCK, December 21, 2007. Tommy reported it to the SF Bureau Office, then the Boston Bureau Office called and he repeated the entire story. While, for **FOUR YEARS,** Blackie continued his vacation with the protection of the FBI, paid for by the people!

Did he pay his taxes? Yes, he is a big piece of crap! For those that are math challenged, since the ROCK sighting that was reported, the Bureau allowed and assisted—protected a dangerous psychopath, sociopath, pedophile, homosexual, to prey on more citizens, in the US and Mexico! Yes, not the guy you want your daughter or sister to date. Tommy has been a CA PI License # 007, for 10 years, Tommy saw RAT, on the ROCK, and whenever he shared it with confidants, they said he was nuts! Well being an Irish Marine qualifies him as a nut, after all, would any of you swim Alcatraz to SF, and the Golden Gate both ways, no wet suit, did not own one!

SEMPER FI!

The ROCK sighting and report of December 21, 2007, by former FBI agent TOMMY TIERNAN was telexed from SF and BN to the BRASS, at BU HQ OC desk. The field was directed by BU OC Supervisor, immediately get them to secret hideout at the GRAND LUXXE, Puerto Vallarta, Mexico, where they had already spent a lot of time. Use the limo from Wilshire, that you used to get them from the ROCK. BLACKIE had complained about missing his BRIO GYM GRAND LUXXE workouts with his trainer. Below is his workout—to keep his heart up to par— that is if he has a heart! Remember—20 plus whack jobs!

BRIO GYM GRAND LUXXE

	MONDAY	TUESDAY	WEDNESDAY	THURSDAY	FRIDAY
8:00 AM	Yoga	Yoga	Yoga	Yoga	Yoga
9:15 AM	Spinning	Spinning	Spinning	Spinning	Spinning
10:00 AM	Zumba	Zumba	Zumba	Zumba	Zumba
11:00 AM	Salsa	Pilates	Salsa	Salsa	Salsa
12:00 PM	Stretching	Stretching	Stretching	Stretching	Stretching
1:00 PM	Abs	Abs	Abs	Abs	Abs
W/RESERVATIONS 5048 5049		HORARIOS/Hours	6:15 AM 10:00 AM		

Yes, since last years bust, give me a Ted Williams Louisville slugger and this RAT B . . . in a cell, and I guarantee a couple HR's over the left field wall at Fenway! We all hope that the novena's come true and this guy croaks soon! Get him in CA, for the James William Lawlor murder, he would join the 725 inmates awaiting to be fried in CA, as literally thousands of victims wait and pray! CA plans to kill the death penalty.

THE WHITE HOUSE

WASHINGTON

October 27, 2004

Mr. M. Thomas Clark
197 Flying Mist Isle
Foster City, California 94404

Dear Mr. Clark:

Congratulations on your retirement from the Department of Justice
after 43 years of Federal service.

Our Nation is deeply indebted to the men and women who devote
their lives to public service. I know how proud your family, friends,
and colleagues must be of your accomplishments.

Laura joins me in sending best wishes for many years of happiness.

Sincerely,

George W. Bush

Conscription

From Wikipedia, the free encyclopedia

Conscription is the compulsory enrollment of people to some sort of public
service. While the service may be of any sort associated with the public, the term
typically refers to enlistment in a country's military.[1] Conscription dates back to
antiquity and continues in some countries to the present day under various names.
Used by the Royal Navy between 1664 and 1814, it was called impressment, or
"the press".[2] Most countries that maintain conscripts now refer to the practice as
national service. In the United States, conscription ended in 1973 but remains
alive in the national memory and is known colloquially as "the draft".

Conscription has historically focused on young men but the range of eligible ages
may be expanded to meet national demand. In the United States, for
instance, the Selective Service System drafted men for World War I
initially in an age range from 21 to 30 but expanded its eligibility in
1918 to an age range of 18 to 45.[3] In the case of a widespread
mobilization of forces where service includes homefront defense, ages
of conscripts may range much higher, with the oldest conscripts serving
in roles requiring lesser mobility. Expanded-age conscription was
common during the Second World War: in the United Kingdom, it was
commonly known as "call-up" and extended to Age 55, while Nazi
Germany termed it Volkssturm ("People's Storm") and included men as
young as 16 and as old as 60.[4] The term of service is often initially set
but includes the prospect of indefinite extension based on national requirements.

Conscription

Military service

National service
Conscription crisis

Conscientious objection

Conscription by country

No armed forces
No conscription
Plan to abolish conscription
Conscription
No information

The underpinning of a conscription system is a belief in the obligations of citizenship; that is, that citizens of a
nation have a duty to support national priorities as well as the rights associated with their status as citizens. As
it is a duty, compulsory service is therefore a supplement to rather than a violation of individual liberties; in
effect, it is the obligation to serve that secures the liberties in question.[citation needed] The extent to which a
population as a whole accepts this premise depends in part on how the selection process occurs -- for instance,
exempting people on account of wealth or political connections undermines the notion of shared sacrifice for
the national good -- and also on the nature of the service.[citation needed] Unsurprisingly, conscription is easier
established and maintained when the moral defensibility of the action is readily accepted by societal values,
such as conscripting troops for time of war when a nation has been attacked or invaded and is considered to be
fighting out of necessity rather than choice.[citation needed]

Conscription can be controversial, because conscripts may have religious, political or moral reasons for
refusing to serve. When governments decide to ignore these objections, protests have occurred and conscripts
have evaded their enlistment by emigrating.[5] Well-constructed selection systems can accommodate these
situations most equitably by providing forms of service outside of typical combat-operations roles or even
outside of the military.[citation needed]

As of the early twenty-first century, most nations no longer conscript soldiers and sailors, relying instead upon

United States Department of Justice
Office of the Inspector General
Audit Division

Audit Report

The Federal Bureau of Investigation's Control Over Weapons and Laptop Computers

August 2002

02-27

J O H N   W A Y N E

9570 Wilshire Blvd., Suite 400
Beverly Hills, California 90212
January 5, 1977

Major M. Thomas Clark
787 Lurline Drive
Foster City, California 94404

Dear Major Clark:

The United States Marine Corps established the history
of Iwo Jima at a time when the American people were in
dire need of the Marines' heroics.

As one of its citizens, I did my best to exploit the incident
in a manner in which the Marines could be proud--at a
time when the little tie salesman was saying they were a
police force that he might disband. I had "Mad" Smith
personally work in a scene in the picture depicting the
time when Forestal went ashore and made the statement
"This assures the Marine Corps for the next 500 years."
The administration would not allow that scene in the picture.

We met the artist that did the monument, had him on the set
when we were reenacting the raising of the flag; but some how
or another, I was not considered when the invitations were
passed out by the Corps for the unveiling. So my position in
protocol would not give you much value for pressure on the
powers that be.

If an opportunity arises while I am in Washington, D. C., I
shall make mention of the situation to the press.

Sincerely,

John Wayne

MAJOR LEAGUE BASEBALL
OLDTIMERS

GOLF
1999
CLASSIC

Cocktail Party

Sunday Oct. 17th, 1999

Park Plaza Hotel
Burlingame, California

BROOKLYN NATIONAL LEAGUE BASEBALL CLUB

215 MONTAGUE STREET, BROOKLYN 1, NEW YORK

Tom Clark
East Side High
All-Essex County – Outfield
Scholarship – Seton Hall

Dear Player:

You have been recommended to the Brooklyn Baseball Club as a
candidate for the Brooklyn Dodger Rookie Stars of Tomorrow.

The players selected for this team will play a series of games
in the Metropolitan area and in the neighboring states. Funda-
mental instructions in baseball will be given to all players
by Brooklyn Dodger scouts, coaches and players. All players
who make the Brooklyn Dodger Rookie team will also be given
awards (Brooklyn Dodger uniform, jacket, cap, etc.).

The day of your scheduled tryout will be Tuesday, June 26th,
1956 at 10:00 A.M. It will be necessary for you to bring your
shoes, glove and uniform with you. This letter will serve to
admit you to the field. Please do not bring anyone with you
as they will not be permitted to enter the park – unless you
live out-of-town and some one member of your family, or one
good friend, has consented to drive you to Roosevelt Stadium,
Jersey City, New Jersey, in an automobile.

If you cannot report on this invitation date, or if you are
still attending school, it does not mean that you will lose
the opportunity of trying-out for this All Star Team. If you
cannot report please get in touch with us so that we can assign
a new date for you.

With all good wishes, I am,

Cordially yours,

Al Campanis

Al Campanis
Scouting Department

AC:mh

P.S. The tryout location has been changed to Ebbets Field, Brooklyn, N.Y.

CHAPTER III

FBI KILLER ESCAPES
DEAD STILL DEAD

THE BLACKIE SURRENDER!!

Tommy is on one of his foreign P I jaunts, to St. Petersburg, looking for the world traveling BLACKIE, and it is "epiphany" time for TOMMY!! POOTIN urged a quick resolution, because Carol is not drinking Russian Vodka!

Now the home stretch. Sources reported that Blackie was Homeland, hunting down Chinese spies in CA, their are many! Rather, sources said his gold plated insurance was based on his being WIRED on all his contacts with the law, for 30 years. He has a Boston Bank library vault full of the tapes, recently expanded to handle the additional tapes and video's, a relative got him a good price. Same deal was setup at the Bank of

Cavan, in case the bureau got to the Boston cache. Blackie says he would be happy to play them at his trial, if the Feds get around to a trial. Or, are they still hoping to bury them with him soon! Don't forget the American Flag, he is an Air Force Veteran.

Was Blackie on the run for 15 years—**NO**! Sources say his handlers at the bureau assisted big time in his days on the lam. He lived with Carol in Santa Monica, five minutes from the LA Bureau Office on Wilshire. They made numerous trips to Puerto Vallarta, Mexico, and other prime spots. Wouldn't you, on a fifteen year paid vacation. Never out of USA—Mexico, for fear of airpot security, unless escorted by a Bureau or contract handler. All this yuk about Europe sightings is just that—**YUK**! And the Air Force Rat, not liking that the ROCK MARINE, made, and reported him, but he was protected by his gold plated insurance! Yes, there was continued silence from J.Edgar's outfit, until the Congressional committees get it, or a Hollywood movie; or Boston Trial!

At the end of this sordid tale you will be privy to the conversation Blackie had with his handler, at table 23 at Michaels that will that will shed further light on—tapes, bust, drunks, psychics, Ranger, photos, Marine Corps pin, trial, and gold plated insurance.

Meanwhile, in Santa Monica, CA, issues were exploding between **Blackie** and Carol. She had been nagging him about going back to Boston and said she was worried about running out of Grey Goose Vodka. He said, great to hear! Blackie said he had many nightmares recently about the Ranger on the ROCK on Dec. 21, 2007. Said he is the same guy he saw at Fess Parker's that summer. Then he made me Dec. 21, 2007, on ROCK, when you yelled "Hey Ranger, where is the book store"? Had we not had the handler at the curb waiting, our ass would be grass! But, the gold plated insurance policy worked. Said he met recently with handler at Michael's to set up the return to Boston.

On Monday June 20, 2011, it was TIME FOR PSA'S featuring Carol to be aired on the View, Regis-Kelly and Ellen. **Blackie** charged her with drinking too much of the Grey Goose vodka on a regular basis. She said look in the mirror you old "fart", I see that every day. The same as the tourist guide who looked like an Irish Marine, not an Irish Air Force, **IRA**—Irish Rat Asshole! Then she started to throw dishes and pans at him, all the time screaming, old fart - # - * - # - #############! Then the dishes flew again!

Your drinking makes you unpredictable, said **BLACKIE,** it may be time to give you the pillow death treatment like you helped me do to **Lawlor,** when we got his ID's. After 15 years, the agency decided they would do 30 second PSA's they had planned, in 14 cities focused on Carol and ask the public to call a local agency, get her and him! But the 14 cities did not include **LA**? Why, the Bureau had the Hollywood type bust planned so their would not be any mess ups with the local press. Then enter the phantom tipster, not local, but Iceland, so press can't interview her, in fact it is not clear if she ever gets interviewed publicly which says the phantom tipster is possibly a phony. BUT, the Iceland lady triggered? the biggest bust since C. B.Winstead took down John Dillinger in Chicago, 1934. The TV spots were on "the View, Regis-Kelly and Ellen". When it aired, "the words and dishes flew again", as Carol said I want Boston, now! With that, the handler should have activated C B Winstead, to blow away **Blackie,** shotgun between the eyes, for all the drug kids he killed. Lt. Col. John R.—MARINE, Mass. State Police would say, **"I'm watching you"!**

Yes, Dillinger killed two police officers in the course of his bank jobs. But was he the one that was killed that night at the Biograph? Some say that Dillinger's girlfriend and Anna Sage "Red Dress", a hooker from England, was about to be deported. They went to the Biograph with Jimmy Lawrence, small town perp from Wisconsin, Dillinger look alike. When CB blew him away, Mel called the ERT for help, no answer. Coroner DOA had brown and not blue eyes; also a rheumatic heart and Dillinger's naval service records said his heart perfect, maybe BLACKIE put in for a transplant! Also, the DOA was much shorter and heavier than Dillinger.

Blackie called a truce, and hid the extra bottles of Goose in his wall with guns/money. Gave her a Goose pop, took one of the agency issued cels to his room and called his handler who was close by, and just up Wilshire from Santa Monica, in Los Angeles. His handler was out, viewing the La Brea Tar Pits, he was a geology major at Penn, on a D-1, football scholarship. So the contact told **Blackie** both of you need to be alive or we can't pull off the **bust**! Your handler will call re details when he returns, be sure to turn in the two cels to one of us, or it could kill us and you, if someone got them. Remember a handler will call you.

Handler called back. **Blackie** told him they needed to close this nightmare off, or he would go broke paying for the dishes, which has graduated to glasses, except for the one she is keeping for her Grey Goose shooters. She refuses to drink from bottle! Also, he hid his guns in the car early this AM while she slept off her hangover! Only had a few guns, if she found them while he slept she could blow his brains out. Handler said we borrowed **50 guns** from **FAST AND FURIOUS** to add to yours,so press will know you really are a bad ass, on the run for 15 years! Handler said we'll be there afternoon—Wednesday,

June 22, 2011 in late PM. Place—1012 3rd St., in basement garage, Not the apt #303, Santa Monica, CA.! The bust will be—**FAST AND FURIOUS!** We will cart away all apartment stuff, including dishes, glasses, booze bottles, broken and whole, etc. We do not want the press picking over anything. Remember, absolutely "no contact with the press"!

Previously noted, at the bust, LA Times reported that the agency confiscated many items, including weapons-50-, cash—$850,000, cel phones, etc. **The cel SIM card**s contain data that needs to be preserved in original form. Given the complicity of the agency in this case, they should be turned over to the Internal Affairs—for safety, and chain of evidence.

Further information sheds light on the 15 year vacation and what he did to earn it! He murdered about 20+ people, including strangling to death two females! What about the countless number he committed to death from drug use, especially in his Southie neighborhood. Yes, we had higher up decision makers, saying he soon will be "sent to the spirit in the sky,"(Atenolol—50 mg), but they were **WRONG!** They were probably **"dodgers"** who joined the peace corps, in the 60's then quit! Unless his 50 mg pill is being shaved down,while he is locked up, so its' potency is lessened, he may live to 90 plus! Or, MK ULTRA will get him.

THE HOLLYWOOD SURRENDER— JUNE 22, 2011—SANTA MONICA, CA

Not sure which Hollywood Director volunteered to direct, film, and communicate the SURRENDER to the world! They did a great **FAST AND FURIOUS,** the shot of the **RAT** in the

orange jump suit was superb! Were the RATS earphones live, so he could continue to tape and monitor the Feds, for playback by the defense. Yes, not only the 16 year vacation, but the bust plan and execution needs a close investigation by responsible law enforcement agents. Maybe you should appoint Tommy Tiernan as head investigator, and IG, given his proven record, on FBI Weapons and Laptop Investigation.

THE NATIONAL ADVISORY COMMISSION ON CRIMINAL JUSTICE STANDARDS AND GOALS

Earlier in Tommy's career he was the key staff person for the Police Section, National Advisory Commission on Criminal Justice Standards—Goals. In that capacity he dealt extensively with the LA COUNTY, Sheriff, Vice Chairman, and Chief of Police, LA, Chairman Police Task Force. The meeting was held at the Hilton Washington DC hotel for 1, 500 criminal justice executives from all over the US with all 50 states represented. The CJSG had been developed by LEAA staff, the conference purpose was to finalize the staff work. This also would update the The President's Commission on Law Enforcement and Administration of Justice (1967).

The conference was three days, the Police group numbered about 350 executives. The conference lasted three days, January 23 to 26, 1973, with a break int the middle, to attend the Memorial Service, at the Capitol for President Johnson, who passed on January 22, 1973. This was about eight years before Hinckley tried to get President Ronald Reagan at the same hotel. If you want to refresh your memory on the report, google it.

For the last night we were busy setting up for the final day of workshops. After a Reception on the Terrace before the Fifth Plenary Session. Presiding was the Administrator of LEAA, Introduction was the Sheriff of LA and Vice, Address by The Honorable William Rehnquist, Associate Justice, United States Supreme Court. At the banquet were about 1,500 conference attendees, entertained by the WDC School Choir while dining on Omaha steak and Chesapeake crab!

The New Jersey representatives included—Capt. Mickey Scheier, New Jersey State Police; Eugene Goss, Executive Director Prudential; Newark Captain Police Ben Gass; James Given, Lockheed—Balclutha, California.

Meanwhile, Tommy was setting up the workshops for the last day, Friday. As he was finishing up, the Matt Kane piper and drummer arrived. The Matt Kane Pub on 13th NW, was a favorite for the Quantico Marines, and the FBI Agents who needed an adjustment from no coffee breaks during the day, and the VOT stress. As soon as the Justice finished, the applause still going, Tommy opened the stage doors behind the head table, announced to no one, but once an Irishman Piper, well! The crowd thought it was part of the program, they loved it, they marched to the end of the stage and came back and off. Again, remember this was a spur of the moment, good, cause the head guy was tear ass! Thanks to the lawyer from the mid-west, who took the blame, had made my suite available to him for counseling sessions with his blanket ladies.

At the party, the LA guy busted in the back door. Said the AG wanted my piper and drummer at his party. Then the AG grabbed my escort, your staff girl, who looked like a Hollywood starlet. While I was getting a pop he said to her, it is time for us to go back to my crib, I never did it to bagpipe music! I had about 20 work shop director's. All from LA Sheriff (Pitchess) or LAPD (Davis). After the banquet, they were all invited to Tommy's suite to celebrate their hard work. No booze from Tommy, not in his budget. They arrived soon after the banquet, all carrying at least a quart or two, not milk!—not IRS!

LA lawmen, many of whom he first met as a Marine Corps Infantry Platoon Commander when stationed at Camp Pendleton in Southern, CA. before shipping out for the Far East (Japan, Okinawa, Philippines, Vietnam, Bangkok, Hong Kong, etc.) Also, as a Camp Pendleton Marine, he saw his Dodgers workout at the LA Coliseum! By the way, his last last pro baseball game before the Far East tour was his old "Brooklyn" Dodgers at the LA Coliseum! **SEMPER FI**!

HOUSE GOVERNMENT REFORM COMMITTEE HEARINGS RAYBURN OFFICE BUILDING

Before Tommy Tiernan retired, his last tour was as the SF DOJ IG. Starting just before the 9/11 attacks, the AG ordered all DOJ components to be investigated for control of weapons and laptops. Tommy was assigned the nationwide review of his old agency. On the day of 9/11, Tommy was off to SFO very early, for flight to Dulles, en route to the FBI Academy, to get sit rep on the investigation. All flights were cancelled, over 3,000 Americans died, the investigation was postponed. The report was devastating and issued in August 2002. Tommy was commended by the AG for the timeliness and accuracy of the of the report, which addressed lots of missing and stolen-weapons and top secret lap tops. The title of the report is, The Federal Bureau of Investigation's Control Over Weapons and Laptop Computers, August 2002, 02-27.

Around this time, Tommy was the recipient of a "Letter of Censure" "Why? not sure BUT—The AG, from 1963 to 1969, received seven military deferments, "draft dodger", while Tommy and his brothers had twenty five-years in the Marine Corps, during the Vietnam era. So, if you have not served, while you say "thanks for your service", you probably have "little respect" for those who have served (draft dropped by the Congress in 1973), as your civilian career moved ahead as a stock broker, Congressman, staffer on the Hill, pro athlete, etc., "draft dodger", well?! . . . **SEMPER FI**!

Tommy had proposed directly to the AG a photo op, for he and his brother, who was retiring. Between them they had served the DOJ for 65 years! During his career Tommy, has awards of performance from six different AG's, and his perp bust at Dupont Circle, from J. Edgar! Also, the bizarre Bank Robbery BUST, of four subjects at the WDC Navy Yard, by drilling MARINES, and Tommy on a Friday AM. Tommy got all the eight MARINES, LETTERS OF COMMENDATION, from J. Edgar.

So, what is the back story. Tommy headed for the Yard, right after getting a Bu car from the NY Ave Bu garage at 0700, some early VOT! At the Yard, was a Marine Captain buddy from Basic Class 5-60, Tommy's class. AND, he always had good 0302 stories about Vietnam, in country. ALSO, he always had a great pot of hot coffee, and no worry about going to BUTTE! While there Tommy checked with the office dispatcher, Terri said all quiet, except for a call re 91 at the Navy Yard! did not say where he was calling from. Tommy hustled to the Bank, a block away, where he was assisted by the MARINES,as they arrested the wheel man, the other three were grabbed near the front and back gates, that were secured when the bank alarm was sounded.

What next? Soon after 45 years commendable service it was suggested Tommy was wanted at Dodgertown—Vero Beach, FL, to rejoin the **Brooklyn Dodgers**! You go figure!

Tommy's reports re Blackie and Carol to SF and BN Bu offices re 12-21-2007, sightings on the ROCK, based on reports, were ignored, misplaced, lost, or sent to the **Moon!**

TOMMY'S PERFORMANCE AWARDS

J. EDGAR HOOVER	MARCH 28, 1966
JOHN W. MITCHELL	APRIL 6, 1971
RICHARD G. KLEINDEST	OCTOBER 9, 1972
WILLIAM B. SAXBE	JULY 11, 1974
BEN CIVILETTI	OCTOBER 3, 1980
EDWIN MESSE, III	JUNE 30, 1985
DICK THORNBURG	JUNE 30, 1989

There were many more awards after the Congress established an Inspector General at DOJ. Which awards does Tommy treasure the most? The one from J. Edgar; the over 100 Law Enforcement Masters Swimming Medals; the AZ-SF and Golden Gate N & S Swims—no wet suit (did not own one), water temp 55°, strong currents, "Great White escorts"!

SUMMARY

Please note this story on Blackie is "reality based fiction" and "inspired by a true story". Tommy's relatives are from County Cavan. Yes, William James, stream of consciousness writing was applied. As for the errors in spelling, grammar and syntax issues, the Nun's at St. Ann's will be excommunicated!

As this case is examined, a theme of conspiracy and/or incompetence may emerge. This is a—protection for information—case that left the agency "shortchanged, co-opted, and comprised". The amount of material to be reviewed is overwhelming! Remember, **Blackie** is many things. **"Stupid"** is not among them! Back in the day, a government lawyer wanted electronic surveillance on **Blackie,** but was told the agency did not tap active informants, too bad! So, **Blackie** wired himself and this may be shared with the world during trial in Boston? Let us remember there are at least 19 dead people, thanks to his serial ways, including two women who were strangled to death by "sissy" Blackie. Also, many lives lost and ruined to meth, coke, etc. from the drugs that made "sissy" millions $, in Boston and Southie! Clearly, the most **egregious** offense was the corruption of public and law enforcement officials from which all of the above flowed!

A few more facts re Blackie as he awaits his trial, now St. Patrick's Day, 2013! To avoid any conflict with **the Marine Corps 237 th Birhday—Nov 10, 2012! Semper Fi!** The US Air Force gave him an honorable discharge? in 1954, having first planned to join the Peace Corps? Later got popped for a series of bank jobs in a number of states—in Indiana, Massachusetts, and Rhode Island, and got 20 years. In AT he volunteered for the CIA sponsored MK_ULTRA program, the goal was mind control drugs—LSD—headed by the CIA chemist administered by Emory University. **Blackie** got caught giving hacksaw blades to a con, so he was sent to the ROCK, November 16, 1959. When the ROCK closed, March 21, 1963, he was sent to Leavenworth, KA, then Lewis burg, PA. In Boston he took over the Winter Hill Gang!

SOME CONGRESSIONAL ISSUES TO BE PROBED BY HOUSE GOVERNMENT OVERSIGHT AND REFORM COMMITTEE

The following are issue areas Tommy suggests for probing, and are not in priority order. First and foremost is the lead agency. What was the management, supervision, reporting, especially down to the handlers. Investigators should not have been a draft dodger! Reason—obvious. There are many in Tommy's generation who opine that the nation would be more prepared for the challenges ahead, if we had a National Service mandated for two years for all citizens. It could be split between military and public service, like we sort of had with the Peace Corps.

BLACKIE—FLASHBACK

Blackie requested "crisis" sit down with Tommy and handler at Michaels, that night. Unknown to them, Tommy first wired table 23, that afternoon! Blackie and Carol just returned from another road trip to Puerto Vallarta, Mexico. Blackie reminded handler of his gold-plated insurance. With the problems with Carol, full fledged alcoholic, he wanted to deal re the future and Boston return. Handler listened. Blackie reminded him he was an Air Force Veteran, handler who probably was a dodger, squirmed and said go ahead. Blackie said he came close to blasting with his machine pistol that damn Ranger on the Rock! Soon after the ROCK, he began to have nightmares, that included him shooting the Ranger. Because the handlers would not help with Bu counseling, Blackie got a psychic, from Laguna Beach, who was gay, to help him through his issues.

You were not close enough in the narrow passage way to see the USMC pin that the Ranger wore, he chose not to blast him cause we need all the Veterans we can get, with the way things are going in the USA. So, as my Hollywood bust goes down in the near future, keep in mind the Ranger encounter is on my tape, and it will be played at my trial, as I tell the jury about my military service! We plan to have Tommy testify also about his MARINE service to the country. Your generation, Jack, does not do service!

Also, the Iceland Tipster—like the Europe sightings, is a bunch of **crap**. She never was heard from in person, she hid more than Blackie. Yes—the cat lady does not exist! She is just another part of the Bu fantasy plan to keep the public in the dark re Blackie. The jurors, will be older and will take up my cause! Also, we plan to show the pictures the Ranger took of our backs with his cell phone, as we passed the book store. This will prove you did babysit us for our vacation, along with other press comments.

OK, last items, a promise to take good care of the drunk! And, I saw in today's paper the big guy will be in Hollywood soon to pick up some more cash, for his third run. As an Air Force Veteran, I rate a seat back East to Andrews more then him, then a hop to Boston, get it done, please! It was great working with you guys for the past 15 years! Please drop by if you visit any of my Fed joints. Yes, I sure hope they send the Guantanamo Crud to the ROCK, single bunk them so they can kill themselves—softly.

TO: ELVIS
FROM: WEST   COAST   CHINA   MILITARY HOMELAND INFORMANT—TOP SECRET

COVER NAME OF INFORMANT—JAMES "BLACKIE" BUTLER aka IRA

Recent indications are:
In near future, China's expanded Armada will take and occupy Guam. Then move on to Hawaii. While there, they will train on their World Class Cats in preparation to take the World Cup in SF.

Plans are set to then move on to Half Moon Bay, CA. The armada will land north and south of Half Moon Bay, CA, "Cancel Mavericks". First off ships will be the bagpipers trained by the Brits in Hong Kong. Next, legions of Gurkha soldiers carrying their Khukuri curved knives—google it. Blackie always carried one on his person. All supported by mechanized vehicles, close air support, drones based on designs the spies stole from the US over the past 25 years. Are the Gurkha's tough, when told they were going to jump behind the Jap lines, as part of a WWII operation with the Britts, they knew the plane was going to come in at tree top level, they just jumped, no shutes!—MALIBU!

Bay area military targets to occupy and control include: Travis AFB; SFO; Moffet Field; Alameda Naval Air Station; Hunters Point Naval Shipyard; Fort Baker; all WWII Batteries for missals developed and secreted in the Dungeons on the ROCK by the spies at specific locations and training, troops watched movie "THE ROCK". POW's that returned were Sean, Nicholas, and Ed, they moved and installed the weapons using solar panels they removed from the ROCK's cell block roof (not effective cause of seagull droppings), which BLACKIE saw when he visited Dec 21, 2007, the day he almost made SWISS CHESSE out of the damn nosey Ranger who said, "HEY WHERE ARE YOU FROM?"—AS BLACKIE WAS WITHIN 2 FEET IN THE PASSAGEWAY, WITH HIS BEADY BLUES—COLD MARBLES, SAYS NOTHING! TOMMY IS NAKED, NOT LITERALLY, no. 357, turned in back at Quantico, VA. FBI Academy. Spies install nuclear rockets north and south of TOMMY'S GOLDEN GATE BRIDGE, after lunch break for chop suey; then the Presido and that movie guys museum; Angel Island—rebuild the WWII barracks and make check with USM's to make sure Lee Morris and the Anglins are not hiding in the tunnels the Mexicans made for the drugs they brought north when "illegal immigration" was finally approved by the National Chairperson, LADY GOGO, SHE MADE OVER FT POINTE AND THREW THE GREATEST PARTIES ON THE ROOF, her personal security was provided by a Ranger, who like Tommy was a MARINE, she said she felt very safe when they snuggled up at night in there sleeping bags on the roof, great views, you guys in Congress should try it!; Mare Island—nuke subs; Fort Mason—docks; OnoSuko AF base; Ft Miley VA Hospital; Palo Alto Medical Center; Travis AFB—for Blackie's 747.

Then time for the occupation to begin. Units move south on US 1, east on 92, then north on 101 to SFO. Along way at all golf courses set up pre-fab barracks, easy to build on flat land, for troops to come, and internment camps modeled after the ones used for the Japs in WWII. Camps retained the 9th hole area for recreational golf. BUT, due to recent gun control laws, golf clubs were ruled a DANGEROUS WEAPON. They were replaced with 2 X 4's, and the golf balls by PING PONG BALLS! Recently reported at the Black House putting green, was the Speaker and his buddy with their 2 X 4's and pingpongs! Extra police have been hired in the hunt for the Florida Fox!

So, what are your plans for the future? If you skip the CUP races, you may consider Conscription, not golf, unless you have ping pongs and 2 X 4's. DD-214's because of Martial Law, will be required by all golf pro's or no golf, so you may as well sign up, many countries have Conscription, i.e. ISRAEL, CHINA, etc. Also, all legislative bodies in US that passed same sex marriage laws, are now beginning the process to do the same for Conscription laws. To protect the same sex marriages, the retired liberal professors, the lib reporters, the lib talking heads, the lib elected types, etc., etc.

PROBE ISSUES—
TO BE ADDRESSED, AND MORE—

— **What is the "back story" on FBI-LA-SA, 5-11-12, LAPD, SA—handler? SA suicide note to wife? Evidence!**

— "Sissy"—BUTLER—is where he belongs, let's hope the USA and team do it right, even though there are issues ahead.

— The 5-14-12 ruling by the Supreme Court because the families sued too late.

Too late, sissy was on the run for 15 years, or about 3800 days, the length of the 9/11 war? What about Ted Williams—Marine?

— The Boston Press (civic responsibility) hit hard at the start, then faded like the Red Sox. Who dragged them into the dugout, Winter Hill Gang and/or Mob?—DOJ—?

— Princess Eugenia Apt # 303, 1012 3rd St., Santa Monica, CA full and complete debrief and report on the "2 cel phones" that were confiscated at arrest. LA Times, 8-29-11, in 8 page report, mentions cel phones 2 different times, and states agents are analyzing them for clues re Blackie calls which may include his call to handlers saying he was ready to **"give up"**! Given the handlers complicity, and to maintain the chain of evidence, the cels should be with the Internal Affairs, make sure all SIM cards have not been tampered with.

— At time of bust reports that Blackie looked sick etc. May well have Carol and Grey Goose Vodka, got her liver!

— James William Lawlor, gave his driver's license for money to Blackie.

Was Lawlor a real person what was his "real" cause of Death?

— Anna, never interviewed re sighting of subjects?
$ 2 mil reward?

When approached in July and September by press, the $2m lady hid in her apartment, if she really exists?, and husband sent email to moon!

— Complete review of Irish Central, 10-21-11, article re case, loaded with significant evidence re "sissy" and carol?

— The ROCK visited by Blackie before he went on lam, claim made by Boston press? How did she know? Got it from Bureau?
"Sissy" served on ROCK for BR. '59-'63?

— Blackie's TOP TEN Poster has 3 photos of him face front, none are profiles?

— Blackie poster, on 4-2-12, inexplicably still on BN Bureau web site?

Full ten months after he surrendered to LA Bureau Agents.

Does this show concern re another escape? Last was 15 yrs.

— On 7-11-11, The New York Post said New Criminals for the TEN MOST WANTED list were needed. Curious why law enforcement waited so long to announce?

— By now it is obvious that law enforcement and press played a role, "big time", in the "Boston Blackie Massacre", worse than the "the Brinks Robbery"?

— ETC, ETC. . . .

15 YEARS REEKS
EITHER OF INCOMPETENCY OR CONSPIRACY

NO LCN MEMBERS FOR ETERNAL COMMITMENT

NINETEEN KILLS—
DRUG OD DEATHS NUMEROUS

Yes, this is stream of conscious writing.

MORE AS THIS STORY DEVELOPS

PS. Not heard at **McSorley's Old Ale House, NY**—but at **Copa D'Oro, Santa Monica,** "since no experienced agents work fugitive or general criminal now, it took 15 years"!

THE BLACKIE FBI 16 YEAR VACATION WRAP

On Wednesday June 22, 2011, about four years after Tommy Tiernan, saw and reported him to SF—FBI and then BN, on the ROCK. On this day Blackie was the guide around Unit 303—surprise? No mention of cel phones that LA Times reported, that SIM cards would show contact with bu to set up "surrender"—have IA check!

Blackie called handler on Friday, before surrender, and all spent all weekend in prep work with PSA's for 14 cities—NOT LA—did not want the locals, but LA Press saw and reported the cel phones.

113

So, Blackie the cold-blooded criminal genius was finished. As the Boston Drug Kingpin, he made $20 M and obliterated the lives of thousands of Southie and greater Boston youth. One was, David LNU, who used for years, at 26 ended it with a S&W .38—Tommy's first issue weapon—back in the day! And Deborah LNU, severe druggie before her whack job.

To help this serial killer stay sharp, he whacked about 40 plus (the rifleman). Who gives a SHIT about the drug deaths, besides the parents and family. Certainly not the investigative journalists because the law enforcement ignored this area too! Mass State Police Lt. Col. would say, "I'm watching you."

Example of IJ focus on Homicides, as compared to concern for Southie youth Drug Addiction. Blackie handled garbage disposal for whacked Ritchie. Kmart donated a sleeping bag. They stuffed Richie in it, put him in trunk of his Jag. Car dumped at beachfront house. Blackie advised co-owner of Squire Lounge he was his new 42% co-owner of the Squire Lounge.

Yes, you will whack Blackie BUT, who is going to take down today's DRUG KING that continues to "obliterate" the Southie Youth!

The Drug Kingpin and trafficking that plagues Boston is replicated in towns and hamlets all over the US. The Mexicans continue to push drugs north to satisfy the US appetite. It is assisted by corrupt politicians, and law enforcement, at all levels. It continues to grow, and the dead drug heads can't stop it—BECAUSE THEY ARE DEAD!

EPILOGUE

This book was written under the pseudonym of TOMMY TIERNAN. The actual author still claims the official reward. He was the first to ID and report the sightings. NOT the Iceland beauty queen four years later, after seeing CNN - PSA re Cathy. Please contact TOMMY'S attorney regarding the reward. He sighted TOP TEN - BULGER and GRIEG, on the ROCK (ALCATRAZ) on December 21, 2007, at 1400, where BULGER did 3 years for 91's - BR's. TOMMY made reports to FBI - SF and - BN, check their phone logs. The Boston call to TOMMY was on Dec 27, 2007, wanting to know what he saw on ROCK the Friday past. Remember, Boston was the OO (Office of Origin), in the BULGER, case, reward $2 Million. No follow up EVER, like when BULGER, slipped out of BN just before his indictment, Christmas of 1994. Hey, I know the old Bureau - and I know things have changed, but not like I encountered! Also sent emails to Bureau and USA locations and SILENCE!

Back on the ROCK, TOMMY TIERNAN (TOMMY CLARK) former FBI SPECIAL AGENT, for NAC - 8 - in training at Quantico, FBI Academy when JFK was assassinated by a Marine, Nov 22, 1963. Back on ALCATRAZ, on 12-21-2007, at 1400, in passageway on north side of the four movie areas, when CLARK saw BULGER and said, "where are you from", which he said to many tourists. BULGER stared back with his beady blues, curled his lip, same SILENT TREATMENT, that the former SA got from the FBI since first report of 12-21-2007. Right then, from behind TOMMY, a hoarse female voice yells, "Hey RANGER, where is the book store"! It is Cathy Grieg, spot on to her WANTED POSTER, distracting TOMMY. WHY - was BULGER on a secret mission? Like when he escaped Boston after indictment in 1994, having showed the FBI the wire he wore in all contacts with the law, pols, FBI and got a 16 yr "gold-plated" insurance! Or, was it CLARK as DOJ-IG-SF, robust investigation of the FBI control over Weapons and Laptops (August 2002 - 02-30) for the Attorney General, for which he got an award!

Please refer to his book for further details. To include the teenager with spina bifida, sentenced to life in a chair, that only wanted to see the "BIRD MAN'S" cell. While you guy's went after the RAT, for WHACK jobs (11 of 19), he walked on 30 years as Boston Drug King. We talk about - FIDELITY - BRAVERY - INTEGRITY - we let him kill Youth and Adults in Southie, by the hundreds - meth, crack, heroin - check with the Boston Health Department, like I did. Who the HELL are the decision makers that allowed this to happen. Probably senior management after the fateful, 1973 Congressional whack the draft job! Just about all the senior levels in the Congress (and staff) and Administration are "blessed" with dodgers. Not true for Ted Williams - Red Sox - Marine pilot in two wars, Warren Spahn - Braves - decorated at Battle of Bulge, and still the winningest lefty ever, Gil Hodges - Brooklyn Dodgers - Marine - invasion of Okinawa!

Recently a reliable source, who has been reliable in the past, corroboratesTOMMY TIERNAN's sighting of BULGER on the ROCK, 12-21-2007. We need the IA, OIG, and probably ISSA's House Govt Affairs to do it, even though they have not done ATF Benghazi. JEH swore TOMMY in, at the main Justice Conference room located on the fifth floor of Main Justice, where the NAZI saboteurs were tried, 6 of 8 were executed, at the DC JAIL, buried in Anacostia, where the Nationals run over their graves!

According to trial testimony, on May 25, 1982, at the meet called by HQ, OC, Supervisor, all this could have been turned around, PROBLEM - no one had the "balls" to do it! So the Winter Hill whack jobs, and the drug OD's all marched on, as the RAT added to his $50 million pot of gold! Where is it now? He had about $800,000 when his 16 year vacation started, when he surrendered in Santa Monica, CA he had $822,000, somehow made money. Plus, a bunch of guns and cell phones, with SIM cards.

In recent past the author left his challenging and exciting career as a US Marine Corps, Infantry Platoon Cmdr; FBI Special Agent; SF DOJ Regional Inspector General.

Your FBI MOST WANTED POSTER says "reward for information leading directly to the arrest of subjects". . . . NOTE: If the FBI had not ignored Tommy's sighting report to the San Francisco office and the Boston office, BULGER would have been arrested on December 21, 2007.

Tommy passed on the info to the Bureau as you see in the book, the Marine part of him wanted to kill THE RAT, but the lump under his topcoat said, I would look like "swiss cheese', no metal detector on the island, no Tommy .357 Magnum! SSA LNU said the perp was proud of his three year stretch on Alcatraz (for bank robbery), and, noted by FBI, "he has vowed that he will never ever go back to prison." This quote was formost in Tommy's mind as he manuvered him in the narrow passageway. Later thought, how could you allow this RAT to wander the country side for 16 years, 19? homicides,—plus and 50 guns! Not sure how it can be done, but you have a creative staff and maybe it is time to flip it! Not sure if your bureau cares, BUT I do, and hope we can turn around this horrid tale. Also, a very reliable and independent source, very close to the case, corroborates TOMMY TIERNAN'S sighting of fugitive on ALCATRAZ on 12-21-2007, which he reported to FBI in SF - 12/21 and BN - 12/27/07.

SEMPER FI!

Ed H—Mark W, both have an interest in the storyline, and attended parts of trial. Movie "Renaissance Man" debuted as the Boston USA was finalizing the extensive indictment for the Boston Drug King—Killer with the help of the FBI. Dorchester was BLACKIE's favorite burial ground. About that time BLACKIE called for a sit down with his handler at Theisman's in Old Town, Alexandria, VA. He told handler he had worn a "wire" and taped ALL his meets with law, pols, and especially the bureau. The quid pro quo would be, you guys hide me for as long as necessary, another words, underwrite my vacation! BLACKIE said his preference was the left coast and Mexico. So he was indicted and disappeared with Cathy. Said all his tapes, and video's were in a safe deposit in Boston with a back up in County Cavan, in case you decided to bust me! The 16 year vacation, lasted until June 22, 2011. The FBI never responded to any sightings, including the one from it's former Special Agent, Tommy Tiernan, on Alcatraz, Dec 21, 2007!

That day was marked by a Mom who runs Tiger Martial Arts, Freeland, Washington. With her was her 15 year old son in a wheel chair, spina bifida, sentenced to chair for life! He had read a lot about the ROCK, wanted to see the Bird Man's cell, they had a flight at 1800 from SFO. Because of holiday, few Rangers, Tommy Tiernan—guide. Had it not been for them, never would have seen the RAT. FBI did not care cause they were half way through their conspiracy to hide the two fugitives for 16 years. Court said RAT had amassed at least $25 Million, and more, in ill gotten gains. The kid and Mom, due a slice, make it happen! Where is the rest, talk to the RAT, and his relatives they know. Better yet, hold the meeting at FENWAY PARK for all the defendants who were "promised immunity", the most in Mass. history, you need venue like Fenway, to hold all of them. Have the Bu Director and the one that he replaced, run the proceedings, with assistance from the HQ OC Desk Sup and the BN OC Desk Sup, who had immunity and took a bullet (?) for the Bu, and is sorry about whack job. Also, consider testimony from the one who said "Who really cares?"

NEWS FLASH - On Marine Corps Birthday the BOSTON DRUG KING sentenced? Murder, none for drug OD's?

See Boston Health Mortality Report - Southie youth obliterated on meth, coke, heroin - provided by BN DRUG KING?

THE RAT made $50 million on drugs, who has money now - not Catherine - how about Winter Hill Gang?

May be time for the press to investigate who directed and managed the RAT'S 16 year vacation?

Did the press or law report he had $ 822,000 in his wall locker (?), in apartment when he "surrendered" in Santa Monica?

Where are the SIM cards and his cell phones from the day they "surrendered"?

Who has the WIRE he used for 30 years in dealings with law, pols, handlers, managers?

What happened to the X - SA who ID'd WHITEY, on 12-21-2007, and called SF and BN, check the phone logs?

FOUR DEAD U.S. STATE DEPARTMENT STAFF

NO INVESTIGATION - NO CONVICTIONS ?

FIDELITY - BRAVERY - INTEGRITY !

YANKEE - DOODLE - DANDY !

STAY TUNED FOR FURTHER DEVELOPMENTS

AND WHAT HAPPENS TO ROTTEN APPLES !

VISIT THE M L KING MEMORIAL

VISIT THE IWO JIMA MEMORIAL !

TO OUR BRAVE SERVICEMEN

WHO VOLUNTEER AND SACRIFICE !

PHOTO CREDITS

The Hall (Seton)
Bay Swims
ALZ to SF
GG Swims
Sharks
Hardware
Navy Yard Bust
AG LTR
Carter—Mondale
Costello LTR
Inaugural—1969
Superior Merit

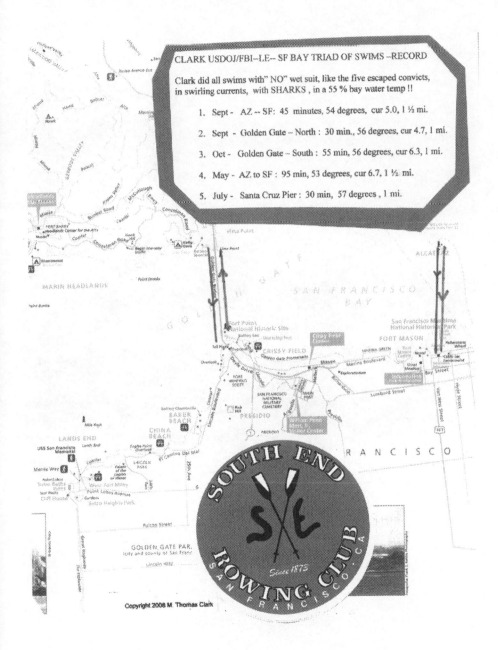

CLARK USDOJ/FBI--LE-- SF BAY TRIAD OF SWIMS --RECORD

Clark did all swims with" NO" wet suit, like the five escaped convicts, in swirling currents, with SHARKS , in a 55 % bay water temp !!

1. Sept - AZ -- SF: 45 minutes, 54 degrees, cur 5.0, 1 ½ mi.

2. Sept - Golden Gate – North : 30 min., 56 degrees, cur 4.7, 1 mi.

3. Oct - Golden Gate – South : 55 min, 56 degrees, cur 6.3, 1 mi.

4. May - AZ to SF : 95 min, 53 degrees, cur 6.7, 1 ½ mi.

5. July - Santa Cruz Pier : 30 min, 57 degrees , 1 mi.

Copyright 2008 M. Thomas Clark

Alcatraz Escape Attempts
1934 - 1963

- 14 Escape Attempts Involving 36 Inmates
- 7 Killed by Gunshots
- 1 Drowned
- 21 Returned
- 2 Returned and Executed
- 5 Still Missing and Presumed Dead
  - 1937: Roe and Cole
  - 1962: Morris and Anglin Brothers
- Only 1 Made it to Shore in San Fran
  - 1962: John Paul Scott

This book is dedicated to the officers and men of the 1st Bn. 3rd Marines, 3rd Marine Division, who served with distinction, as a part of their country's force in readiness.

July 1961 - Sept 1962

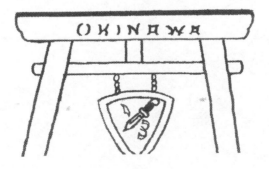

OKINAWA

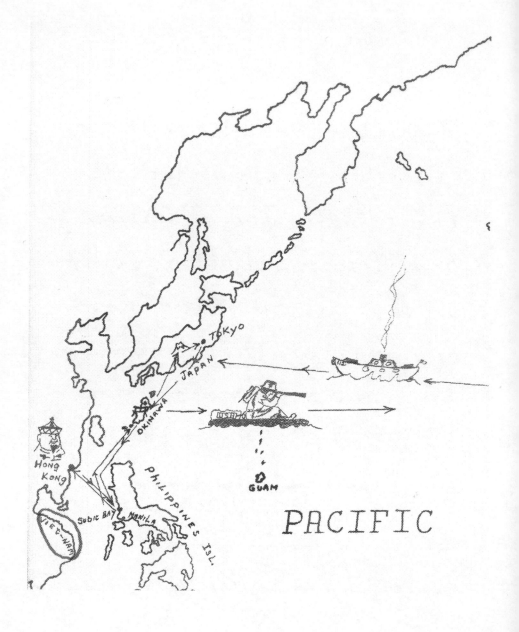

J. R. Rosetti

1000 Westchester Avenue, White Plains, New York 10604

March 13, 1973

Dear Coop,

I just can't tell you how appreciative I am over the performance of Tom Clark at making the conference the success it was, but of greater import in the final analysis was his work in the overall efforts of the Commission.

As you may know, when I was given this assignment, the National Advisory Commission's work was far from complete and it was our responsibility to tie together the loose ends, develop and the appropriate standards and goals for the conference, and synopsize all that transpired as of that date. To this end, Tom Clark single handedly is responsible for what I believe is the best part of the report and that is the section relating to police. In addition to this work, his ability to relate and understand police types regardless of background is a real plus to what LEAA is attempting to do.

My experience and yours would normally suggest that conferences are "nice places to go." It is now six weeks since the conclusion of that conference and from where I sit and the feedback I am getting, I see for the first time criminal justice standards and goals as a reality. I believe, though somewhat prejudiced, that the efforts of Tom Clark via the conference were responsible for this renewed effort that is needed at this point in time in the life of LEAA.

I would hope that you could convey my sincere appreciation to Tom Clark and you can tell him for me that in retrospect, the "bagpipers" don't sound so bad.

Best wishes,

Joe

Mr. Cornelius M. Cooper
Regional Administrator
Law Enforcement Assistance Administration
U. S. Department of Justice
1838 El Camino Real (Suite 111)
Burlingame, California   94010

CARTER - MONDALE
TRANSITION PLANNING GROUP

P.O. Box 2600
Washington, D.C. 20013

December 17, 1976

Dear Mr. Clark:

I got your card and note regarding the obstacle course record at Officers Basic School at Quantico, Virginia. When were you in Basic School? I was there in the summer and fall of 1960 in Officers Basic Class "2-60".

As for your suggestion that we run the course again, I'm going to need a lot of practice. Unfortunately, my schedule for the last several months has not permitted me to do much physical exercise, and I sadly confess that I am not in very good shape. Maybe if we set a time in the future to run the course it would inspire me to start working out. Lord knows I need some inspiration.

Warm personal regards.

Sincerely,

Jack H. Watson, Jr.

Mr. M. Thomas Clark
Regional Administrator - Region IX
Law Enforcement Assistance Administration
1860 El Camino Real - 3rd Floor
Burlingame, California 94010

PATRICK J. COSTELLO
RES. 388-4935

Lawrence and Costello
ATTORNEYS AT LAW
LAWRENCE BUILDING
ROUTE 3 — HIGHWAY 61 WEST
RED WING, MINNESOTA 55066
TEL. 612-388-7139

STEPHEN A. LAWRENCE
RES. 388-7237

February 1, 1973

Mr. M. Thomas Clark
Law Enforcement Assistance Admin.
U. S. Department of Justice
1860 El Camino Blvd.
Burlingame, California   94010

Dear Thomas:

I generally do not expend my time writing letters, especially
to male types, but in this case I had absolutely no choice but
to write and let you know how much I enjoyed working with you.
It was one of the best situations I have ever been involved
with, and I feel alittle like a "prima donna" receiving as much
of the credit (both bad and good in the case of the bagpipes)
as I received.

Thomas, believe me, it will be an experience I will remember for
the rest of my life. Thanks.

                              Best personal regards,

                              Patrick J. Costello

PJC:kms

P.S. Have you heard anything on
a follow-up? Let me know
if you want some help or the
letters on the pictures. O.K.

Inaugural Committee ★ 1969

The Pension Building · 440 G Street, N. W.
Washington, D. C. 20025
Telephone: Area Code 202 · 386-6501

J. WILLARD MARRIOTT,
Chairman

ROBERT G. McCUNE,
Executive Director

January 2, 1969

Mr. M. Thomas Clark
69 Rockridge Lane
Woodbridge, Virginia

Dear Mr. Clark:

It is my pleasure to inform you of your appointment as a member of the
Safety and Security Committee of the Inaugural Ball Committee, 1969.

The Inaugural Balls will be held on Monday, January 20, 1969 at five
Hotel locations and the Smithsonian Museum of History and Technology.

You have been assigned to the Smithsonian Museum of History and
Technology.

Please report to Thomas Rasmussen, Dep. Chief, Ret. in charge of the
arrangements at 7:30 P.M. at the above location.

As soon as possible I will furnish you with a set of general instructions as to your duties.

May I take this opportunity to thank you for your willingness to
serve as a member of my Committee and I am sure it will be a most
pleasant assignment.

Dress for the assignment—Black Tie.

Sincerely,

Howard V. Covell

Howard V. Covell (Asst. Chief, Ret.)
Chairman, Safety and Security Committee

HVC:jm

Roster
of
Superior
Merit

Tom
Clark

In looking through the list of past East Side High School graduates, we find very interesting, generous, and courageous people. One such person is Tom Clark who graduated from East Side High School and lived most of his teenage years in the Ironbound section of Newark.

While at East Side, Mr. Clark already showed signs of stardom by setting two Newark high school swim records, and being part of the All-City Baseball Team. This man's determination to succeed gained him great recognition through his various travels all over the country and his real-life activities. There are life stories that have an uncanny similarity to fiction books. Fiction characters participate in exciting and perilous adventures where the hero survives and receives an award as well as great honor. Tom Clark's life resembles that of a fiction book hero. After ESHS Clark continued by going to Seton Hall University on a baseball scholarship and becoming the captain/MVP of the swim team. Although college taught him a lot it was being a Major in the U.S. Marine Corps and serving in the U.S. and the Far East, that taught Tom Clark courage, readiness, and the skills he needed to become an FBI Special Agent. All cases in which Mr. Clark has participated are important to him, since each taught him a lesson. However, there are cases which he will always remember as the most important, cases such as the JFK Assassination, the Jimmy Hoffa case, the Florida East Coast Railroad Train Bombings, the Mississippi Civil Rights Killing, the Martin Luther King Assassination, and numerous bank robberies and fugitive cases.

Dedication and determination have been the main motivation throughout Tom Clark's life. These traits have gained him various awards in both his career and beloved sports. Mr. Clark has been honored with awards from six different Attorney Generals, the director of the FBI, and the Immigration Service/Border Patrol Investigation. To Mr. Clark, though, the most important awards he has received were for swimming. Swimming has always played a prominent part in Tom's life. Being the first Justice Department Official to swim Alcatraz to San Francisco and Golden Gate Bridge both ways and winning over a hundred swimming medals in the International Law Enforcement have proven to be the most special recognitions for Tom.

Tom's life is full of great accomplishments and boundless recognitions for his efforts. However, he has never forgotten his beginnings and where his story book life started. East Side holds many special memories for Tom and he has gladly come back to encourage new graduates. He wishes the class of 2000 the best of luck, and encourages them to never give up on their dreams.

FBI KILLER ESCAPES

TOMMY TIERNAN

THE ROCK

EAST COAST IRISH TWINS WORKED FOR J. EDGAR

INSPIRED BY A TRUE STORY

The day on the ROCK was icy cold,
just before Christmas when
Tommy Tiernan, the hard-bitten
US MARINE came face to face with
"BLACKIE BATTLER – KILLER"!

ISBN13 Hardcover: 978-1-4797-6766-5
ISBN13 Softcover: 978-1-4797-6765-6
ISBN13 eBook: 978-1-4797-6767-6

Published by Xlibris
Order Today!
Orders from your local bookstore or
call toll 888-795-4274 Ext. 7876 order online at
www.xlibris.com, www.barnesandnoble.com,
or www.amazon.com

Xlibris